The Secret Journals of Nell Clarke

Lynda Earley

The Secret Journals of Nell Clarke
Copyright © 2022 by Lynda Earley

All rights reserved. No part of this publication
may be reproduced, distributed, or transmitted
in any form or by any means, including
photocopying, recording, or other electronic
or mechanical methods, without the prior
written permission of the author, except
in the case of brief quotations embodied
in critical reviews and certain other non-
commercial uses permitted by copyright law.

Tellwell Talent
www.tellwell.ca

ISBN
978-0-2288-8434-7 (Hardcover)
978-0-2288-8435-4 (Paperback)
978-0-2288-8433-0 (eBook)

*For
My
Family*

Journal One

Wedding at Waterloo Mill and the Journey, 1903 - 1904

June 25, 1903 Waterloo Mill, Dorset, England

I am just beginning to write in the journal which Mother gave me for my birthday last week. It is a delightful book with a leather cover and a small lock and key. It is not a diary with the days marked in, but a book of blank pages which invite longer stories. I hope to fill it with my secret thoughts and observations. My favourite book is "Little Women" by the American author Louisa May Alcott. Jo March is my favourite character. She is lively and adventurous and she aspires to be a writer. Recent events in my life have opened my heart to love and adventure. I plan to fill this journal with detailed descriptions of my sister's wedding and the life-changing events which preceded it.

****

The early morning sun sneaks through the lace curtains of our bedroom window beneath the gable, surely a good luck sign for my sister Mary's wedding to her sweetheart James. Soon the bustle and chaos of this day will begin: all of us, my four sisters and I must be dressed by 11 in our elaborate wedding costumes, the corsets, the petticoats, the wide hats, the satin overskirts, those tight pinching laced up shoes. Mary's gown is very complicated, with hoops, ribbons, veils. My three brothers have less to prepare but there are still many boots to be shined and suits to be pressed. Mother will soon be scurrying through the house in her most worried state, cross with the maid, and with us. Father, in his usual stoic way, will be sitting outside somewhere, smoking and hoping for it all to be over.

A wedding is such a special day. What will Mary be feeling when she awakes? She still sleeps peacefully in the narrow bed beside mine, but I know she was up very late with last minute preparations. She has been "stepping out", as they say around here, with Walter North for what seems to me to be a very long time – almost three years. He is ten years older than she is and at thirty two has already established himself in his father's clothing shop in nearby Gillingham. He seems terribly dull to me with his mutton chop whiskers and pale grey eyes. However, I suppose she sees him differently? Again, as I do so often, I let my mind slip into my favourite daydream: my own wedding and the man I imagine as being by my side on that special day.

His name is Albert Edward Townsend and he is is the most handsome man in the world. He has piercing blue eyes, a rather sharp noise, wonderful hands. I have thought of little else since he came to stay with us last month. He and my brother Will became friends when they were fighting in the same regiment in South Africa. He spent a week here at Waterloo Mill before they both left for London to make preparations to emigrate to Canada. What stories they had to tell! The Boers, the Blacks, the horses, the heat, the lack of food, the plagues of insects. How brave they must have been, fighting for their country and the empire! I overheard Will tell Father that of 525 fine boys who went out, only 210 returned after the war. The rest were invalided home or died. A copy of the official photograph of their regiment, the Middlesex Mounted Rifles, is now is our sitting room where I can sneak a look at it often, to remind myself just how handsome Bert is and to assure myself that he is real and not a figment of the overactive imagination of a nineteen year old.

Bert Townsend, second from left, back row

Bert and I had very little time to talk and absolutely no time alone, yet I hope that perhaps he also felt some attraction to me. It was very difficult for me to act normally in front of the family as we shared meals and evening visits because I felt so overwhelmed by his presence. I calmed my excitement, hoping it wasn't obvious to my parents, although I think that Mother may be observing the change in me. I was able to listen to his stories, although he was rather quiet, perhaps shy because we are so many.

He too comes from a large family who own a large farm in Somerset called East Harwood. He is the youngest son and therefore will not inherit any land, which is the reason that he and Will are going to try their luck at homesteading in Canada. They say that there are large tracts of land available there for hardworking farmers who are willing to settle in a place called the prairies. Will had made inquiries and found out that they could go from London to Brandon, Manitoba for ten pounds. They know almost nothing about Canada, except that empty land stretches for hundreds of miles and that the climate is very harsh. They are young, strong and adventurous and so they have gone to Canada. Of course they are also men. I am young, strong, and adventurous as well, and am skilled as a seamstress. I love he idea of emigrating; I feel so stifled by life here. Should I follow Will and Bert to Canada? How else will I make my dream of marrying Bert Townsend a reality?

I let my mind drift back to that wonderful day when we went on a picnic beside the Innis River during Will and Bert's all too brief week with us. Mary and her sweetheart, Will and Bert, and our youngest brother Lot, who is only eight, and I were able to fit into the buggy to embark on an outdoors adventure. Our lively pair of horses took us along the back roads until we reached a wide grassy place to leave the horses and the buggy. Will unharnessed Prince and Lady Anne from the buggy and the rest of us unloaded blankets, table clothes, baskets of food, and flasks of tea which we had helped Mother pack earlier that day.

We walked along the river in single file on the narrow path treading carefully as the river was flowing fast after the spring rains. I was walking in front of Bert, and once, unbalanced by my heavy wicker basket, I slipped. Bert reached out to steady me and and for a brief wonderful moment his strong hands were on my waist. Suddenly, in front of me I saw Lot wading into the water, splashing toward the shallow part, where he used rocks as stepping stones to the path on the other side that led to the farm where his friend Nicholas lived. I knew the currant would be too strong for him if he went in too far, so I cried out, afraid that Lot would be carried away by the cold rushing water. Bert and Will quickly pushed past me and waded into to the knee high-water. They grabbed Lot by both hands and helped him up the slippery bank. Although they had very wet boots and trousers, they were laughing at their adventure.

We continued slowly as the way was sometimes muddy, and we had to dodge overhanging branches of yews and beeches. Soon we saw the sunny opening ahead, the picnic clearing. This place has always been special for our family; as children we called it our fairy ring. We spread out the blankets quickly. Will, Bert, and Lot took off their boots and socks and were soon drying off in the sunshine. I would have liked to be sitting beside Bert, but it just didn't work out that way as Will and Lot were there, on either side of him, playing games which involved wiggling their toes in the sun!

Our picnic spot seemed magical that day, truly a Fairy Ring, full of bird song and fresh breezes. Were there ants or stinging nettle, mosquitoes or hard jagged pebbles beneath our blankets? If so, I didn't notice them. My eyes and ears were for Bert only.

We set out the picnic, freshly made bread, butter churned that morning, individual veal and ham pies, tiny new potatoes cooked in their skins, and a selection of cheeses. We had strawberries and cream for dessert, and yes, in the bottom of the dessert basket, my favourite, tiny butter tarts with currants! Mary unpacked plates, cups, cutlery, the flasks of hot tea and we all quickly put food onto our plates.

Mary commented, "These veal and ham pies are wonderfully delicious.! Why does everything taste better when eaten out of doors?"

Will looked up from eating long enough to say, "Melt in your mouth tarts as usual. I'll miss these in Canada. We'll be cooking for ourselves over there, Bertie!"

"Can't be any worse than the food we had in South Africa, Nobby!" Bert responded, using the nickname my brother had picked up during the war. A very curious name – I long to ask its origin but somehow I know that it is one of those "men's secrets" I am not to be privy to.

I really wanted to ask Bert more about their time in the war, just so that those blue eyes would turn my way, but Walter wanted to know more about Bert and Will's plans to homestead in Canada. The conversation involved talk of horses and crops and how farming in Canada might be different from what Bert was used to at East Harwood. Will of course knows nothing of farming. Our father is the mill operator and we have little land, just enough for a small garden. What will he do in Canada, I wonder? The two of them are being very brave, striking out to a new land.

The long mid-summer afternoon gave us time to linger after our meal. Mary and Walter, the young lovers soon to be man and wife wandered off to spend time alone. Lot, Will, Bert, and I poured more tea from the flask, relaxing in the dappled shade. At last I had a chance to talk to Bert! Shyly, I asked Bert to tell us more about his family. He talked quietly about his mother, his sisters Jane and Beatrice and his brothers William, John and Len. He slowly and with some hesitation began to recount his very first memory when he was three. Bert said: "I was in the back orchard with my "darling" nurse, Sally Webber. I saw a lot of things flying around in a swarm. They were settling on an apple tree, and I picked up a stick to poke them with"

He paused and looked at us as if wondering if he should share this personal childhood story with people he had just met. I offered some quiet words of encouragement: "Please do continue!" Seemingly more at ease now, he went on.

"Sally screamed in fright, 'Bobo, come here!" She was pulling at her tousled hair, crying her eyes out. The things were flying around me but they did not touch me. I wondered why didn't Sally come to rescue me. I thought better about using the stick, and ran to darling Sally, hoping for a kiss. Alas, no kiss. She grabbed me and ran to the house. She put me in my mother's welcoming arms. It was a good thing for dear Sally that the flying things did not sting me as they were some of grandpa's bees in swarm."

I was intrigued by this story which told me a little about this man who intrigued me so: his lack of fear of the bees, his attraction for darling Sally. When he said the words "hoping for a kiss", my imagination leaped toward all sorts of possibilities.

Lot had been listening quietly to this story, and when it was done, he blurted out the question that was also in my mind: "What about your Daddy?"

So Bert began what was probably the central story of his childhood. At first haltingly, and then with more confidence, he settled into the relaxed spirit of the surroundings, leaned back on his elbows and in that wonderful quiet voice told us about what happened when he was twelve. He began:

"The 29th day of July that year -1897 – was a very hot day. John and I were hoeing turnips, although I would have preferred to be with Father, who had gone to the

Meet of the Staghounds at the nearby estate of Venniford. I was a bit worried about him as the mare he'd taken was hard to handle; she sometimes held the bit in her teeth and bolted. As the sun began to slide below the nearby hills, I tried to reassure myself that Father was a competent and very experienced horseman."

Bert's voice wavered a bit and the breeze rustled through the leaves of the grove. I leaned forward, anxious to hear every word. He took a deep breath, and looked down at his hands. I could see that he was clasping them tightly, trying to stop them from shaking.

Finally, he was able to continue. "I returned to the house. and rested by the front gate, waiting for Father to return for supper. Dusk was settling in and I began to feel very uneasy. Father should have been by now! I peered into the increasing darkness and was just able to recognize our neighbour Lawrence Tudley as he rode slowly up our drive. He dismounted and asked to see Mother. I could tell from Lawrence's demeanour that something very serious had happened. I ran into the house and got Mother from the kitchen where she was busy with supper preparations. She and I went to the door, and Mother invited Lawrence to come in. He declined. He appeared to be very ill at ease, anxious to tell his story as quickly as possible. Standing there in our front step, hat in hand, clutching the reins of his horse, he told us that as Father and he were coming home from the hunt another neighbour, William Chapman suddenly climbed over the hedge beside the road, darting out in front of them. Father's horse became frightened; she turned short and bolted.

At this point in his story, Mr, Tudley was overcome with emotion and had to gather his thoughts before he could bear to tell us the rest.. He explained that Father was unseated, falling from the saddle to the rough stones of the roadway. His words went something like this.

"I dismounted quickly. Dear Bert was lying in a pool of blood on the cobblestones, I bent down to him and realized that his head had struck a very sharp rock. Mrs. Townsend, I must tell you this. He looked up briefly, then his eyes, rolled back in his head. Although I tried, I could not revive him. People are coming soon with his body."

My mother and I stood there in shock, speechless and dazed. My mother fainted and I caught her in my arms."

We all sat very silently as Bert shared finished his tragic story. Quietly he continued.

"His death was such a shock to us all. I for one was dubious about Chapman's story. He and Father were not on good terms and Chapman was a mean customer. At the post-mortem and inquest he was cross questioned but no blame was laid. However, just before I left home for South Africa, we heard that he had admitted to friends that he had frightened the horse on purpose to give father a scare."

Our silence continued after Bert's story as we each shared his immense sorrow in own way. I realized tat that moment that he was a natural born story teller! I wondered if he was also a reader, or had the fact that he was forced to leave school so young ended his time with books? I love to read, and spend many hours with the few leather bound books we have inherited from Grandfather. How wonderful it would be to share my life with someone who loves the world of literature!

It was also clear from hearing Bert talk about the land that his pride in being a farmer and his close connection to the land are very important to him. I suddenly had a vision – shimmering and unclear, a premonition perhaps? Fields of golden grain as far as I can see. Bert in the middle of it, dwarfed by the immensity of the landscape. Is this be a glimpse of the Canadian prairie? Will I eventually share his life? I feel an overwhelming. desire to join him there on that far stretching prairie……to be with him always.

****

My daydream about the picnic ended abruptly as Mary suddenly sat up in bed. "What time is it? I've overslept!"

We heard Mother's step on the stairs and the frantic edge in her voice: "Girls – get up! So much to do before we go to the church!"

We both moved quickly: dressing gowns wrapped around us, we descended the steep stairs to begin this most important day.

Our household was a fury of activity as we got into our wedding finery. So many layers! I had been wishing for the cool weather we usually have in June, but the heat had already begun before we all walked to the church, fortunately a short distance from our home at Waterloo Mill. My corset was too tight, my new high buttoned boots pinched my feet and my hat was too heavy with its rows of tulle and artificial flowers. Although the service was beautiful, it did drag on and I felt faint; Reverend Wilkinson was slow moving and slow talking. The highlight of the service were the vows. Walter mumbled his vows and hesitated in a few places, but Mary looked radiant as she spoke out clearly, her voice shaking only slightly. The kiss was brief, then down the aisle they went, out into the bright sunlight to begin their new life.

Immediately after the ceremony, Mr. Wesley Corbett, the photographer from Gillingham, asked us all to gather on the drive in front of the mill for the family wedding picture. Photographers coming to the wedding was a fairly new idea; previously the wedding party had to travel to Gillingham to Mr Corbett's studio for a formal photograph, but innovations in photography have lessened the cost for photographer to come to the home or church. Adding colour to photographs was a new innovation. Mr. Corbett was a small village photographer and not yet familiar with that technique. I had also heard people will eventually be able to buy small cameras to take their own photographs, too amazing to be true. Perhaps it's just a rumour!

There were eighteen of us and it took some time to get organized for the portrait. Arranging us in a formal manner, Mr. Corbett seated Mother and Father on straight-backed wooden chairs from the kitchen. Mother looked quite elegant, but rather austere, in her dark green velvet dress with its intricate lace collar. Her hat was the latest design, a cloche, I think it is called. Gold chains adorned the front of her dress. She didn't often have occasion to dress in such finery and had given weeks of thought to designing and sewing all of our dresses, a gigantic task which consumed much of her time in the last few months. Father looked very stern and somewhat uncomfortable in his best suit and waist coat, leather gloves in hand, black shoes highly polished. How different he looked; I hardly recognized him! I had seldom seen him out of his heavy work clothes. Father worked long hours grinding grain for farmers in the Gillingham area which did not allow for much leisure activity or for the clothes that go with such pursuits.

We gathered around our parents in our finery: Lot, my youngest brother, was in the back row, looking very young and rather nervous, Beside him stood Hubert with his wife, Alice, in an elaborately flowered hat. My sister Beattie was positioned beside me, tiny and more plainly dressed than the rest of us. This was her choice: she is so shy that she never wanted to draw attention to herself. On my right was my handsome brother-in-law, Jack Fern. his hand resting on the chair in front of him, where my sister Lou sat in her red velvet dress with their baby Bill on her lap. Luckily, the baby was intrigued by the camera and therefore quiet. Dolly, Jack and Lou's six year old daughter, the flower girl, also stared directly at the camera, looking a little self-conscious in her in wide brimmed hat with the satin bow tied under her chin. Her long sleeved dress was made entirely of lace and she carried a basket of delicate primroses and showy white daisies. Nora was the bridesmaid. The photographer placed her beside Walter and Mary. She looked lovely in her pale blue silk dress in the shockingly short fashion with her tiara of ribbons and flowers. Her dress was mid calf length showing off her dainty ankles and stylish shoes.

"Centre stage", of course, was reserved for the bride and groom. They looked very serious. Walter's moustache and hair were groomed to perfection: too perfect for my liking. He stood tall and proud in his stylish dark suit, his top hat in hand. Arrogant is my word for him! Mary looked beautiful, though a little tired and pale. Her veil framed her face in such a way that she looked quite angelic as she walked up the aisle of the church. I loved the flowers in her huge bouquet: daisies, forget-me-nots, yellow roses and a beautiful trailing vine which reached nearly to the hem of her dress. Mary's dress, which Mother spent long hours creating, was fashioned of white silk overlaid with Cornish lace. White wedding dresses have been the fashion since Queen Victoria got married in white. Mother told us that when she got married her dress was navy blue. Brides wore dark colours and veils were unheard of. I had helped Mary dress, so I knew that her corset, called an "S" bend, was tight, designed to make her waist look tiny and to push her bosom up and out to show to advantage. The sleeves of her dress were wide at the top, tapering down to a narrow cuff at her wrists.. When Mother was making the dress, she told us that these are called Gigot sleeves, a style that came originally from a French designer. How fortunate we are that mother is such an accomplished seamstress. I hoped someday be able to design and sew as beautifully as my mother; and be able to make a living doing it. Perhaps in Canada. What a dream!

The sun was hot on my face I and was glad that my wide brimmed hat shaded my eyes. My satin dress which I had loved while it was being made was not designed for comfort with its tightly cinched waist and stiff petticoats. I was relieved when we were finally arranged to Mr Corbett's satisfaction. He took several photographs and the session was over.

We had a few minutes to relax before walking to the nearby Gillingham Inn, located about a half a mile downhill from home. About forty guests gathered in the dining room which Father had rented for the occasion. Father's salary as the master of Waterloo Mill must be a generous one, although admittedly I know little about the family finances. The dining room looked looked splendid: white lace table clothes, set with Royal Albert "Lavender Rose" bone china; bouquets of pink roses with surrounded by ferns sprigs of lavender matched the design of the china. What a romantic setting!

The meal was a traditional roast beef dinner with all the trimmings. To be honest, I was too exited to pay much attention to the food. The three tiered wedding cake was the "Grand Finale". Mother had spent hours making and decorating it with elaborate rose and lavender designs in the icing. Mary gazed lovingly into Walter's eyes as he placed his hand over hers to cut the cake.

The speeches were short and jolly, as everyone was anxious to move out of the stuffy, somewhat crowded dining room into the bricked courtyard, where we danced under the stars to the melodies of a local orchestra. The four musicians are friends of the family and play for weddings because they love to participate in such a happy occasion, although I know that Father will give them some financial reimbursement as well.

As I watched Mary and Walter dance the first waltz together, I thought of Bert and my plans to emigrate to Canada. This idea very often occupies my mind, almost consuming me at times. I am anxiously waiting for a letter from Will with more information about where he and Bert had settled, if indeed they had found a place in that vast country. It has been two months with no news, but I realize communication is slow across the Atlantic, and I have no idea how a letter would travel in Canada. My imagination paints a picture of a dust-filled trail with a horse and rider galloping over long distances, but the picture is vague and unformed. I don't know enough about Canada to paint clear pictures in my mind. The geography, the people, the weather, everything is a mystery. Thoughts swirl in my mind: very frightening, but exciting as well. I have never travelled more than a few miles from Waterloo Mill, and my acquaintances are all connected to my family and a small area around Gillingham.. Finding information about Canada is very difficult. The only information is contained n the advertisements in local newspaper about homesteading there. I don't ask many questions because I'm not ready to tell my family about my plans. Questions, questions, questions, so many questions. Will I have to go to London to apply for immigration? How long will the process take? Where do the boats leave from? How long is the journey? When I get to Canada, will there be quarantine? I try not to dwell on all the situations that will face me because I want to remain strong in my resolve to undertake this adventurous journey. Once I arrive in Montreal, more questions come to mind. How far will it be to the prairies? Will I travel by train? What about money? How much will it all cost and where will the money come from? I make some money as a seamstress but I work mainly for acquaintances who hear about my skills by word of mouth. My savings are pitifully small, a few pounds tucked away under my mattress. The unknowns are worrying: last night my mind was so crowded with these questions that I lay awake for hours. Mother inquired about my health this morning, saying that I looked tired and haggard. It is so hard to keep these plans secret! Sometimes I despair that my dreams will never become reality, but then I remember those blue eyes, those strong hands, his wonderful voice and swear to myself: I will be with him even if I have to travel half way around the world!

May 16, 1904 on board to CPR steamship Champlain

I want to record my thoughts as I begin to make my dream of joining Bert in Canada a reality. The ship is still in but port, but I have settled into my cabin and want to do some writing now in case I am seasick once we begin to move!

This is only my second entry in my journal. I have been very busy this past year since I wrote my long story about the wedding and the picnic that still burn vividly in my mind. I have not taken the time to write. I also lacked the inclination to write as long as my plans remained dreams. Gradually, however, my plans began to turn into actions. Mother very reluctantly accepted that I was determined to make this journey and although we never discussed the matter, she my have realized that my main motivation for going to Canada was not to be with my brother Will. Father was also very quiet on the subject, but from the winks and smiles he gave me I knew he was excited for me and understood my desire for adventure. Did he guess my underlying reason for this journey? I'm not sure, but he helped me fill out immigration papers, got the correct signatures, and mailed the package to London. The the whole process went smoothly, perhaps because Will was already in Canada with employment and had written to support my application to immigrate. Father also gave me some money for the journey.

I've done it! Incredibly, I am now on board one of the first CPR steamships making the Atlantic crossing from Liverpool to Montreal. I'm in a second class cabin which Uncle Lot prebooked for me. He refused to tell me the price, but I insisted he take the few pounds that I managed to save from my seamstress jobs. Uncle Lot explained that the Canadian Pacific Railway Company's entrance into the steamship business has increased completion and lowered the cost of fares. In fact, the cost of travelling in steerage has been cut in half, in what Lot calls the "Steerage Wars". He predicts that the CPR'S plans to build more steamers will begin a "Golden Age" of this kind of crossing as the new ships are able to make the trip across the ocean much faster: ten to twelve knots an hour, although I'm not at all sure what that means. Our journey is estimated to take about two weeks or longer, depending on weather conditions.

May 21, 1904

I have been so sick that I have barely left my cabin. I have met no other passengers and know only the kind face of Edward, my porter, who takes away buckets and brings food which I cannot eat. He says the trip has been very rough due to strong winds and much rain. I can't sit up to write and want to save these wonderful white pages until there is no longer danger of vomiting all over them!

May 30, 1904

On board the CPR TransCanada train, from Montreal, Quebec to Virden, Manitoba

My ocean journey was delayed by bad weather in Halifax, but there was no quarantine when we reached Montreal and I was able to board the transCanada train the next day after spending the night in a small hotel recommended by my friendly porter. He told me that Montreal is a very exciting city but of course I have no inclination or money to be a tourist on this journey.

Most of my transatlantic journey is a blur due to my seasickness, and alas, most of this incredible rail journey has also passed without written record. I have been so fascinated by the vistas rolling by my window for the last few days that I have not found time to write during the day and there are no lights in my carriage at night. We have left the rocky shores of Lake Superior and on now the vast expanse of the Manitoba prairie. Almost there!!

I have been sleeping soundly after my restless days and nights on the ship. Fortunately, I find the gentle swaying of the train and the clicking noise of the train tracks quite calming. I have also spent a lot of time chatting with my fellow passengers, who are mostly British and European families travelling to the prairies to begin a farming life. There are no women travelling by themselves, and most people I have met in the dining car are amazed that I'm travelling alone. The food is wonderful and is served in style. I am enjoying the meals very much after being able to stomach nothing but crackers and tea on the week long ocean journey. The staff are very friendly, and one of the porters has been telling me that the completion of the trans Canada railway a few years ago has made a huge difference to the settling of this vast land, especially on the prairies.

We will be in Virden in few hours. In the dining room, I have been sharing a table with Robert and Elizabeth Parham, a friendly couple from Dorset who are also going to Melita! They are planning to hire a horse drawn carriage to take them the 40 miles south to Melita, a few hours journey on a dirt road. They assure me that there will be room for me and my trunk. Robert and Elizabeth have friends who recently immigrated to Melita and tell me that once we arrive, we will have no trouble contacting my brother Will.

Journal Two

Melita, Manitoba, Canada 1904 - 1913

April 13, 1904 Melita, Manitoba, Canada

The long journey is over at last. I have been here only two weeks and tonight I walked to the edge of town to gaze out over the fields in the twilight. I have found a fairly comfortable place to sit on the blanket I have brought along, and want to take some quiet time to sort out my feelings about this brand new country of mine in a brand new diary which I bought at Dodd's store. It's not as elegant as my first diary which I filled at the end of my long rail journey. However, it suits my new surroundings, with its light green cover and its practical lined pages.

Such a different landscape to the one I have left behind in Devon. I have already heard stories of the opening up of this land. The earliest settlers walked up to 100 miles from the nearest railway in Brandon to reach the land they had chosen for their farms. This land that I am lost in was recently covered with herds of buffalo and a tribe of Indians called the Mandans rode their horse between encampments on the river. I have never seen a buffalo or an Indian! Will I ever get used to Canada? Do I really want to make it my home forever? Will I ever see my family again?

I have made my farewells to all those dear faces. My long journey across the ocean, and by train from Montreal to Melita means that weeks of exhausting travel are now behind me. I am here, somewhat settled. My mind is full of doubts, but I must continue to be brave. Somehow the physical journey seems less complicated than the journey still before me, to somehow see Bert Townsend and let him know my feelings for him. I realize that perhaps I have been fooling myself that Bert will return my love. But at least I know he is in the same country.

    I have been very fortunate since my arrival here. I was able to stay with Will in his tiny rented house. People have been friendly and welcoming. Most of them are recent immigrants from England and are empathetic to my situation. I found a job and a place to live almost immediately. I am working in Dodd's General Store and keeping house for Mr. Dodd. I have my own room, and Mr. Dodd is a kind old bachelor. The work in the store is quite easy and I love meeting the people who come in to buy items. They can't grow or raise themselves on their farms, everything from tea and sugar to bolts of cloth. Of course, townspeople are also customers and they buy more items. Bread, butter, and cheese are the most popular items. Now that spring is here the shelves are full. Mr. Dodd explained that there are often limited deliveries during the winter months. I have heard tales of snow drifts ten feet deep and minus forty degree temperatures. Will I be able to adjust, accustomed as I am to the gentle rains of the Devon countryside? I also hear stories about the heat of summer days and plagues of grasshoppers and mosquitoes. I am not at all sure what grasshoppers are, let alone what plagues of them will be like. Melita is quite a small town of about 500 people. It is located in the south western corner of Manitoba on the banks of the Souris River. The river valley offers a welcome break with its shady trees. However, it can also be menacing. Last spring when the snow melted the river overflowed its banks and the surrounding flats filled with deep fast flowing water. The townspeople speak sadly and quietly in the store about the death of Ed Thompson, who was attempting to ride a horse over the flats and drowned. The townspeople had to use boats to cross and it was July before the water subsided completely.

The streets of the town are lined with maples, still bare but which I imagine will offer cool shade as summer progresses Carragana hedges have been planted around many properties and they too will soon be showing their leaves. I was shocked at the barrenness of the spring here, but everyone says it will be beautiful by the end of May. The nights seem very cold to me and sometimes the winds during the day sting my cheeks. This evening is mild and the prairie seems quite benign and somehow friendly. Perhaps this will become my place on the earth after all. We lived close to the earth at home; maybe my dream of a home with Bert, owning our own farm, growing our own food, having children is not so outlandish after all.

When Will's letter arrived last fall, ending months of anxious waiting and prompting me to begin my journey, he said that he and Bert had been working together on a farm outside of town owned by a Mr and Mrs. Brimson. They found the work hard and the pay was low for "green" workers, $15.00 a month. They were up at 5 AM and in the fields ploughing by 7. They were laid off for the winter months so they went to work in the woods quite far north of here. It was axe work and log hauling, the letter said, with hard labour from daylight to dark. They had their dinner out among the trees about three miles from camp.

They considered it good work for the winter, as the pay was $30.00 a month with free room and board. They are expected back here soon, but unfortunately a late spring blizzard has delayed the trains. My long wait continues.

June 19, 1904

It's my twenty first birthday, certainly a milestone in my life! I wish that time would pass more quickly. I want something to happen with Bert. Yes, Will and Bert have been back from the north for a few weeks. I have seen Will often. He has decided bush work and farming are not for him and has rented house in town close to Dodd's store. Will is slim of stature and finds the days long and the physical work hard. He is hoping to be able to work with the solicitor in town. Before he enlisted and served in South Africa, he spent a year working in Gillingham, helping with wills and property transactions. Although he has no legal training, he hopes one day to open his own office as a notary public. This term is not used in England and therefore sounds rather strange to me. However, Will says it is considered a position of prestige in small prairie towns like Melita.

Bert is working on the Brimson farm once again and Will says he is enjoying it.. Will has told me that Bert has a girlfriend in Somerset called Lillian and that they write to each other. The transatlantic mail is very slow; surely it must be difficult to conduct a meaningful relationship that way? I wanted to ask Will more questions but I felt too shy to do so. I am reluctant to confide in him about my feelings for Bert. Our family is reticent about discussing such personal things.

Will and I have been meeting in the evenings at Lee's Chinese Cafe on Main Street. It's a quiet place and its booths offer privacy for conversations. We sometimes have supper there. Chinese food is a completely new experience for me! Lee's speciality is chicken fried rice; at first I was dubious and ordered the ham and mashed potato instead. However, Will convinced me to try it. To my surprise, I liked it and now order it regularly.

Last week, I finally found the courage to ask Will if he could go out to Brimson's farm and invite Bert to join us for supper. He said yes! Will and I arrived at the cafe before he did and sat at our favourite booth. I made sure that I sat facing the door so that I could see Bert as the door swung open and he walked in. He was as handsome as I remembered. He saw me immediately and for a brief second those blue eyes met my gaze. He sat down beside Will, across the table from me. My heart pounded as he reached across to shake my hand.

"Welcome to Canada! I know from experience, how long and hard the journey must have been! You are very brave to have come by yourself. How are you settling in?"

My voice shook a little as I answered, telling him briefly about getting my job and about how friendly the townspeople have been. Lee came to take our orders and we convinced Bert to order the speciality as well. Will and

Bert began talking about what they had both been doing in the last few weeks. The weather, crops, horses, people they both knew in town were the topics of conversation and I was too shy to join in. Our supper came quickly as there were only four other customers in the cafe. Like me, Bert decided he was partial to chicken fried rice and we all finished our plates quickly. After dinner, the conversation turned to the differences between food here and in England.

"Certainly, there is more variety here. No Chinese cafes in rural England!" Bert exclaimed.

Will pointed out that there were many similarities as well because most of the immigrants in this part of Manitoba are English who cook food that is familiar to them. Since we were discussing food, I decided to mention the magical day of the picnic when Bert had visited our home in Devon.

"The last time we shared a meal it was in a very different setting" I said. Both Bert and Will knew I was referring to the picnic and we began to reminisce about the events of that day and about our families in England. Will became quiet as Bert and I talked. Perhaps he was beginning to see that I was interested in Bert? Did I see a spark of interest in Bert's inquiries about my family and my journey here? Perhaps he was just being polite?

Our time together was too soon over. Bert stood up abruptly.

"I must get back to the farm. Mr and Mrs. Brimson will be expecting me. Will, I'll see you again soon. Nell, it's been wonderful to see you again. I'm glad you decided to join us in Canada."

I murmured my goodbye, trying to hide my disappointment in his departure. I had hoped that the long June evening would allow him to stay in town for a longer visit. I had let myself envision him asking to walk me home. Instead, Will and I left the cafe shortly after he did. I walked back to my lodging with Will, glad of my brother's company, but still wishing the evening had ended differently.

As I climbed into bed last night, I was consumed with doubt. Has this journey been in vain? Will Bert arrange for Lillian to come to Canada? Will I become a spinster in this forlorn place, a maiden aunt to nieces and nephews? My pillow grows wet with tears, and I am unable to sleep. I look out my bedroom window, longing for sunrise even though the sun has barely set. Negative thoughts swirl around and around in my mind. My body grows tense, my hands clench. I long to get up and begin my busy day of work at the store. Dawn will still my rambling thoughts. In daylight, hope will return.

July 15, 1904

Brimson Farm

I had not seen Bert again since meeting him for supper at Lee's Cafe. As the weeks went by, I was beginning to despair of ever realizing my dreams. Then something happened that raised my hopes. I heard women in the store gossiping that the farm where Bert was working needed a girl to work in the house. I realized that if I was going to get closer to Bert, I would have to take matters into my own hands. The next time Mrs. Brimson came into the store, I steeled myself to ask her about the position.

As she was about to leave the store with her groceries, I said, "Mrs. Brimson, I'd like to talk to you." Fortunately, there were no other customers in the store: I told her I had heard that she needed help on the farm and quickly added,

"I am interested in working for you. I have decided I would like to get out of the town and try something different, perhaps closer to my rural lifestyle in Devon".

Mrs. Brimson and I had become friendly during her visits and I knew her as a motherly type whose two grown daughters have married farmers and now had places of their own. She replied, "As you may have heard, my youngest daughter Isabel married just a few weeks ago and I decided that without her at home, I need help with the cooking, cleaning and gardening as well as the few farm chores that Mr. Brimson considers suitable for women. Although I know it is common for women on neighbouring farms to help with the milking, Mr. Brimson will not hear of it, so you will be helping only in the house. To be honest, I'm lonely without Isabel, and I'm looking for companionship as well. Do you think you would like that kind of work?"

I answered "I am very experienced with housework as I helped mother with a large household in England, and I would look forward to being your friend as well."

After Mrs Brimson and I talked for a few more minutes about practicalities, it was obvious that she liked me. She said. "Nell, I'd really like you to come to the farm and start as soon as possible."

I was ecstatic! I was a little hesitant about telling Mr. Dodd about my new plans, but that very evening I made myself be brave. I told him I would be leaving at the end of the week. Mr. Dodd was sad to see me go, but he said that he would have no trouble finding someone to take my place. I moved out to the farm on the weekend. Fortunately, I have only a few possessions, and it was easy for Mr. Brimson to pick me up with the horse and buggy and drive me the few miles to the farm. I have a comfortable room at the back of the farm house and already I feel quite at home here.

Bert is very hardworking. He milks fourteen cows every morning and night and works in the fields as well. I am disappointed that there is little chance to spend time with him. Fortunately, Mr Brimson does allow women one task in the barn. Mrs. Brimson and I go out to the milking shed and clean the separator in the evenings and I am able to see Bert for a few glorious minutes. The "Boss", as Bert calls Mr Brimson, brings out the hot water from the house and carries the cream back. While we wash the separator, I am able to chat with Bert, mainly about England. He seems interested in what I have to say but he is a bit tentative and shy. He is very surprised that I have emigrated on my own and has asked many questions about my long journey here. I have told him about all the difficulties I had convincing my family to allow me to follow my plan. I have also told him about the terrible seasickness of the long ocean journey and the nights spent tossing and turning in the narrow bunk of the enclosed cabin. He of course had had all the same experiences, although he didn't get seasick. We talked about the tediousness of the long railway journey across Canada, especially along that long rocky shore north of Lake Superior. We also talked about the importance of the railway to the growth of Canada as a country. It has opened up the prairie to immigrants like us. We also share the good experiences. We have many pleasant memories: friendly people, the excitement of seeing forests, the Great Lakes, the prairie. The wildness and the immensity of Canada have thrilled us both.

In these conversations I have not even hinted at my real reason for making this life changing journey. Will I ever be able to share these feelings of love?

Mrs. Brimson and I get along well, almost like mother and daughter. We have had many conversations about Bert as we sit by the stove sharing cups of tea in the evenings. I have begun to hint at my deep feelings for him. I have also told her that I am worried that he doesn't share these feelings. She says quietly:

"Nellie, you must consider that Bert thinks of himself right now as "the hired man" and may feels he's not worthy of your attention."

"If only I could share my feelings more openly."

"Don't worry, dear. If it's meant to be, things will start to happen. Believe me, I remember when I first met Tom, the problem quickly became how to stop things from progressing too rapidly!" She laughed quietly as she said this.

I have only a vague notion of what she meant, but I know that my feelings for Bert include a strong physical attraction. We have had very little physical contact but I still remember the thrill of his hand on my waist as we walked into Fairy Ring for that magical picnic when I first met him in England. What are his memories of that day, I wonder?

August 12, 1904

Mrs. Brimson was right. I have been so totally immersed in love that I have had no time to think. It has become very evident that Bert does share my feelings. Because of our conversations and because of what she called "the charming glow" that comes over me in Bert's presence, Mrs. Brimson began to go back up to the house in the evenings, leaving me alone with Bert in the barn. Our conversations have become more and more personal, even intimate, and our physical attraction has overwhelmed us both. I was shy at first and so was he, but we quite quickly became comfortable with each other. Mr. and Mrs. Brimson are sometimes out in the evenings and when we have all the chores done, we sit on the front steps of the house, excited to be near one another. Bert has started calling me "Darling Nellie" and has assured me that Lillian, so far away in England is "losing out". As he looks at me with those intensely blue eyes, I believe every word he says.

Some nights we join the Brimsons for a game of cards in their kitchen. We play a game called "Nap" which involves having partners and taking what they call "tricks". We usually pair up "ladies against gents." Mrs. Brimson says that if she plays with her husband there'll be constant bickering. Bert played the same game in South Africa and is very quick at it. Our family were not card players so I am slow to learn, but Mrs. Brimson is patient with me as her partner:

"Don't worry, Nell, you'll soon have beginner's luck and we'll be taking all the tricks!"

However, the longer we play, the more I become distracted by Bert's knees which are in constant contact with mine under the table; surely I am not imagining the gentle pressure I feel constantly! I blush and my heart beats so loudly I was sure that everyone could hear it. I often miss an obvious play, and when I catch Mr. Brimson winking at Bert, I am even more embarrassed. The card playing is fun, but for Bert and me, it is really just another occasion for us to spend time together. The Brimsons obviously realize what is happening between us. Although they never say so in so many words, I think they are enjoying watching Bert and I fall in love.

Other evenings Bert and I take walks in the pasture, enjoying the long prairie twilight. Our conversations are becoming more personal, more intimate, and occasionally he takes my hand or puts his arm around my waist. Such a romantic atmosphere, with the horizon stretching on forever,. This is the life I imagine sharing with Bert. The tiger lilies are just beginning to bloom at the edges of the field. I love them, with their boldly orange colour and their deep cups and long stamens! They seem so sexual to me, a thought I would not have had a few weeks ago!

The Brimsons have three horses which are usually in the pasture when we take our evening walk. Bert talks lovingly of the horses he had growing up at East Harwood. He is an experienced horseman and tells me stories of his successes at the Taunton Horse Show. His horses often won first prize. Although we never had horses at home, I seem to be drawn to them now. I particularly like the young roan with the blond mane that Mrs. Brimson calls Jumper. I sometimes take an apple from the kitchen or a carrot from the garden as a special treat for him. I stroke the softness of his nose as he munches, and Bert stands beside me so close that my whole body burns with an overwhelming desire to be even closer to him. I dream of the day when we can have horses on our own farm.

As the summer continued, until one night, as the twilight lingered over the fields, in the middle of a conversation about our families in England, Bert blurted out:

"Nellie darling, you look so sweet and lovely tonight. May I have a kiss?"

We both stood up and we were in each others arms and those first passionate kisses changed us from friends to lovers. I can't bring myself to write about the details of what has happened between us, but we have managed to spend a lot of time alone and we are both totally absorbed with our feelings for each other. Although Brimsons don't speak about it, I know their silence means approval.

I don't know what the future holds. We talk often about our dreams of having our own farm and Bert talks of an engagement soon. He wants to get enough money together for a ring. I keep telling him I don't need a ring but he insists. He has asked me so many times about my favourite gemstone that I have finally told him that I love sapphires, so he says he will go to Brandon soon to buy a sapphire ring, perhaps set with small diamonds. He has already written to Lillian and told her about me and about our plans to marry. We will write our families soon and set a date for the wedding.

<u>None of this seems real – I exist in a haze where only the times Bert and I spend together stand out crystal clear in my head. We are obsessed, consumed by love.</u>

Lynda Earley

Underhill Farm October 15, 1906

I have just found my journal in the bottom of a dresser drawer - the one I bought at Dodd's store and planned to write in regularly to record all the important moments of my new life in Canada. Alas, it's been almost two years since I have had the time or inclination to write anything. I have not recorded some very important events as they happened. I doubt that my writing of them now will have the same intensity as my last entry here, written and underlined as it is in dark black ink. I have allowed many events to slip away unrecorded, although I hope to find some time to write now that we are more settled on our own place. Granted, it's not really our own; we rent it from Jack Underhill. The house is small but comfortable enough for the three of us. I enjoy having my own kitchen, although the old wood stove is sometimes uncooperative and I have had a few charred disasters. However, I am gradually learning to bake bread, pies, and cakes. I also am beginning to prepare big meals that Bert likes. I have a small garden, with lettuce and carrots. I even have some tomatoes. Most of all, though, I love the animals. We have five horses, two milk cows, three heifers, two pigs, forty chickens and two geese, "for a start" Bert says. The horses are my favourite. I especially love Dolly, the spirited blood mare which Bert bought especially for me. He broke her himself to ride and to drive, and we are able to put dear baby Lynda in the buggy and go to town to get groceries at Mr. Dodd's store.

I also buy material at the store. Last Christmas, Bert surprised me with a very special present, a brand new

Singer sewing machine, the latest model with a fine oak cabinet. I have no idea how much it cost, probably more than we should be spending. He must have ordered months in advance and hid it in the barn until Christmas morning. When we were courting, I confided in Bert how I had been developing my seamstress skills before I left England and how I would like to someday supplement our income with a sewing business. I realize now that my life on the farm is so busy, especially with Lynda to care for, that the business may never happen. I will always be able to make my own clothes and will save money that way. I have already made some wonderful outfits for Lynda, including a special "party dress" of red velvet with lace at the neck and cuffs. I enjoy making my own patterns and choosing suitable material. Although the choice is limited in the store, Mr. Dodd has allowed me to make some special orders. I dress plainly myself, but I am planning to make a white silk blouse with long puffed sleeves, a high neck and some delicate lace on the bodice. I also have plans for a long brown velvet skirt, fairly full which seems to be the fashion now.

It seems a long time ago that I worked in Dodd's store, before Bert and I became lovers, before I began to feel the stirrings in my womb, before our rushed and very private marriage in the lawyer's office with only brother Will and Mrs. Brimson as witnesses, before the birth of darling Lynda May. So many experiences crowded into a few short months. Such a range of intense and contradictory emotions I feel overwhelming love for Bert, but I also suffer from the guilt and shame of my pregnancy. I suffer from telling the lies which I have allowed and which I know will follow me through life. We have decided to tell Lynda when she gets older that we were married a few months earlier and we have already lied to our families in England about Lynda's birth date. Of course, some people here know the truth. Perhaps as time passes that knowledge will fade? Of course, the circumstances of our marriage will never fade from my memory and sometimes when we go to church my guilt is almost too strong to bear. Being in that little Anglican Church reminds me of the church in Gillingham and the happiness I saw in my family's faces during Mary's large wedding there a few short months before I came to Canada.

Enough of the past! I must concentrate on the present, on making a happy home for us; otherwise the past may consume me.

Our first year on this rented farm has been difficult: our first crop was not good because we had hot winds that ripened the grain too quickly. Bert said that our oat crop was good but that the wheat yield was down by half. This was unfortunate as wheat prices are sixty cents a bushel while oats are only twenty five. We didn't make enough money to pay all our debts. One third of the profits had to go to Jack Underhill for rent and we had to pay for threshing and harvest help. When Lynda was born, Bert hired Mrs. Brooks to help in the house and Annie Hodgson came to help cook for the threshing crew. I wanted to do more to help, but I was confined to bed for a few weeks before Lynda was born and was in bed for a few weeks afterward. Although the birth itself was relatively easy, and Lynda is a big, healthy baby, Dr. Byers says I have a "delicate constitution" and that we shouldn't plan to have a large family.

Two weeks after Lynda was born, I was finally able to join Bert at the supper table. We were enjoying a cup of tea after dinner and Mrs. Brooks was "reading our cups" She sees images left by the tea leaves in the cups and is able to predict happening from their shapes and connections. She said she could see little of interest in Bert's but when she looked in mine she exclaimed:

"My, what a commotion! What is it... a cyclone perhaps?"

We all immediately went over to check on Baby Lynda in her cot. She was sleeping soundly, so we stepped out on the verandah to check the weather. A hot wind was blowing hard from the south. We looked over towards the barn where the hay and oat sheaves were stacked. Huge clouds of dark smooth smoke billowed up into the sky and we could barely see the barn itself. Bert ran across the yard, disappearing into the haze of smoke. He let all the animals out of the barn, which luckily was not on fire, just the sheaves beside it. Sparks had flown over from the threshing operation at Ernie Goodlands farm which was next to ours.. The sparks from the steam engine on the threshing machine had started a fire in the field there. Ernie came over with a team of horses.

I heard him shouting through the smoke: "Bert, where's your plow? I am going to plow some furrows between us as a fireguard".

Bert motioned to the plow and soon they had it behind the team. He started off. Nothing happened!

"God "he said, "the ground is too hard and dry!" Then Bert shouted, "Just a minute – I forgot! I took the shares off to sharpen them – they're in the granary!"

It took precious minutes to put them on, but soon the furrows were plowed, and the men stepped back to assess the situation. The actual fire never crossed the small creek between our properties. The barn was safe and the house was far enough west not to be affected even by the smoke.

Bert washed up and came in for another cup of tea. "Nothing was burned and no harm done", he said as he settled into his chair. "But I will definitely be paying attention to Mrs. Brooks' tea cup reading in the future!"

October 30, 1906

Yesterday, I took Dolly to town as we usually do on Saturdays. Bert always goes with me, but he was busy doing the fall farm work, so this time we both decided that I was ready to make the trip without him. Dolly handled well as we drove into town. I was very proud to be doing this on my own, with Baby Lynda happily cuddled in her basket beside me. I put Dolly and the buggy in the livery stable while I did my shopping. We spent some time in Mr. Dodd's store, and he and I chatted as he went through my list, helping me find the essentials that I needed for the week. While we were there, a few of the local women came in. Emma Tilbury seemed to glare at us and did not speak to me. I sensed her strong disapproval about Lynda's quick arrival so soon after our wedding. Fortunately, Martha Andrews was also there and was very friendly. She commented on Lynda's dimpled cheeks.

"How healthy and contented she looks!" she exclaimed.

I know that Martha and John have been married for five or six years. Perhaps Martha is wishing for a baby of her own. I tell myself that I should feel only joy about Lynda and try harder to bury my guilt. I am not sure I am capable of hiding my feelings, especially at night when my mind dwells on the sinfulness that I allowed to overtake me.

Later, we walked down Main Street to visit Will in his new office where he is setting up his business to sell insurance and do simple legal matters. He greeted me with a wide smile. I settled in the wicker chair in front of his desk and put Baby Lynda in her basket on the floor. She was sleeping soundly. I was very happy to have a chance to visit with Will.

"Nell, I'm so happy to see you! I have very exciting news. Cissie has finally been able to book her passage to Canada!"

He was referring to Cecilia Dickinson, his fiancee in England. She has been working as a lady's maid in one of the big houses outside Gillingham and has been to Europe several times as a companion for Lady Wilson. Her employers have been trying to convince her to stay with them; they tell her she is one of the family. However, she has decided to leave all of this for Will. Love has once again won out over practical matters! I know Cissie only slightly because her home is quite far from Waterloo Mill. Will and Cissie's courtship was brief, interrupted first by Will's time in South Africa and then by his immigration to Canada.

"What great news!" I exclaimed to Will. "I liked Cissie so much the few times she visited our home. When is she coming?"

"Next spring. We are going to be married, probably in June, as soon as we have time to plan the wedding. I am hoping to rent a little house on Elm Street for us."

We chatted for awhile longer before a potential customer interrupted us. We left to go to the stables to get Dolly and the buggy to go home. I walked along the narrow path beside the street, avoiding all the horse droppings, and carefully carrying Lynda who was beginning to stir from her nap.

I began to imagine Will and Cissie's wedding in our little church. It will be beautiful and perhaps she will ask me to be her matron of honour. Cissie will look wonderful in white with her reddish blonde hair and delicate white skin. I can't help the jealous feelings that creep into my mind, knowing that I have passed up forever my chances of a proper wedding. Fortunately, it's not a long walk to Ernest's stable, and soon I was too absorbed in the business of getting ready to drive home to dwell any longer on my feelings about Will and Cissie's wedding.

Ernest harnessed Dolly and helped Lynda and I into the buggy. I handled the reins confidently now. The trip to town had gone so well that I was sure the trip home would be uneventful. We got a few blocks down Main Street but as soon as we turned the curve that leads out of town, Dolly reared up, took the bit in her teeth and began to gallop for home. I tugged with all my strength but she didn't slow down. I was sure the buggy would tip over. I was terrified and so afraid for Baby Lynda.

The terror was short lived, thank God. I saw a man on horseback flash by the buggy, He grabbed Dolly's harness, and after running along side for a short distance, was able to rein her in. I was shaking with fear, but I managed to gather my composure to thank my rescuer, a man I knew only by sight. His name was Doug Davies; he worked in the carriage shop where Bert had once taken the buggy wheels for repair.

"I was just going to my house for lunch, Mrs. Townsend, but I have time to accompany you home just in case this fine horse of yours has running on her mind!" Mr. Davies recognized me, or perhaps our horse and buggy, so he knew that our farm was only a mile up the road.

I gratefully accepted his offer. As we drove into the yard, Bert was just coming in for his lunch. When he heard the story of the runaway, he thanked Mr. Davies profusely and invited him in for lunch.

"My wife is expecting me. I have to be on my way. I am glad to have been in the right place at the right time!"

Bert helped us from the buggy and looked anxiously into Lynda's basket. She was smiling and gurgling. Her reaction to our adventure was obviously much different than mine!

Bert grabbed me in a huge hug. "Next time, Nell, I will take some time off to go with you. I can't stand the idea of you and Baby Lynda being in any danger!"

I have mixed feelings about the events of this morning: on the one hand, I am so thankful the runaway ended positively and grateful for Bert's concern, but I hope that he will trust me to take Dolly on my own again. I love the feeling of independence and I so enjoy being with Dolly. She is so beautiful and strong and I know that Bert bought her especially for me.

November 15

I can barely stop my tears.. After my misadventure in town, Bert and I have had several serious and sometimes heated conversations about whether or not we should keep Dolly. Bert keeps repeating versions of his reasons why we must let Dolly go to someone else.

"I admit that Dolly is the smartest driver we can ever hope to own, but she is idle much of the time. She is too fine boned and delicate to be used for farm work, and too young and skittish. Her idleness makes her hard to handle and I will never feel confident letting you take her to town on your own, especially with Baby Lynda in the buggy."

Another evening as the debate continued, he made me feel very guilty by saying:

"In the spring, when I will be spending very long hours getting in the crop, I need you to go to town regularly. There will be butter and eggs to take in to the creamery and other chores to do. I won't be able to take the time to go with you and you need a dependable, reliable horse to take you to town to do these errands."

I pleaded with him, using my arguments for keeping Dolly. I kept telling him, "Surely with time and practice, I can learn to handle her. She is beautiful and gentle most of the time. She is my favourite animal on the farm!"

Just then, I looked out the kitchen window: Dolly was galloping around the pasture, rearing slightly as she came to a corner and changed directions. Her neck was arched and her mane flew in the breeze.

"I can't imagine this place without her!"

He put my around my shoulders and said, "Yes, she is beautiful, but look at her run. As I have been saying for the last two weeks, she's too spirited for you to handle! I have strong feelings for her too and I will hate to see her go. Nell, I need another farm horse. Pat is the very first horse we ever bought and he will make an excellent driver. He's easy to handle, and a good trotter. Few can pass him."

I knocked his hand from my shoulder and broke away from him. "So this is really what it's all about! You need another farm horse! What about my needs!! I need Dolly's spirit and beauty. I need the feeling of independence she gives me! She was your special present to me. Your words were so loving and promising when you brought Dolly home!! Why have you changed?" My voice was cracking now, and I realized that I was nearly screaming.

"Calm down, my darling. We can't always let our emotions rule our actions," Bert said quietly. With that, he left the house, and I saw him walk slowly towards the barn. I knew then I had probably lost the argument. And I knew also that Bert was referring to the other times before we were married that we had allowed our emotions to rule our actions. I wondered for the first time if we would be married now if I hadn't become pregnant. I tried to shut that thought from my mind; dwelling in the past will only make me sadder. I realize that Bert's arguments are logical but I still had a faint hope that he might have a change of heart.

This morning, without a word to me, he left the house and I saw him ride out of the barn on Dolly. Two hours later he returned on a huge roan horse, wide of girth and very tall. He looks sturdy, strong, old, dependable, and quite ugly, in other words, Dolly's opposite in every way. My heart fell. I knew I would never see Dolly again on this farm. What had he done with her?

He soon came in, looking rather sheepish but happy at the same time.

"Darling", he said, "I got an offer the other day from Matt Coates to trade Dolly for a big work horse, and the deal is done. "Old Bob" is ten years old and a very reliable worker. In the spring, I plan to get more horses, and then Pat can be your full time driver for trips to town. We will miss Dolly, but what's done is done."

I looked at Bert, and unable to stop my crying, I ran into the bedroom. Bert followed me, saying "I'm sorry, Darling, but we have to be practical if we are going to be successful in farming. Matt Coates knows Dolly because as you'll remember, we bought her from his bother Jim. He gave me a good deal. Please understand that I had to do this."

I didn't respond right away, angry that he'd made all these plans without consulting me or even telling me about them. Surely I should have some input into decisions like this? I could see my beautiful Dolly being driven into town on Saturdays nights by snooty Lily Coates in their fancy buggy, although perhaps she won't be able to handle her? I hope that will be the case!

Later, over cups of tea and some currant cake, Bert and I made up, but I have a sadness in my heart, not only for the loss of Dolly, but for the realization that Bert's blue eyes have a steeliness to them that I had not noticed before, and that his love for me does not include seeing me as an independent woman. My decision to follow him in Canada, my long solitary journey her are in the past: I am a farm wife now, with all the confines which this kind of life requires.

July 24, 1907

I have not written since Dolly's departure. I do not like to record sad times and the winter was long and harsh. Bert and I have been awkward with each other since he traded Dolly away. Both of us seem to realize that it has changed our relationship; we don't talk with the easy camaraderie that we once both felt so strongly. However, spring thaws and warm winds bring renewal and we both have thrown ourselves with enthusiasm into the hard work of the spring season on the farm.

Bert rented another half acre to the north of us. He put in ninety acres of wheat and summer fallowed the rest. True to his word, he got more horses in the spring. He traded Prince for two horses, one a mare in foal we call Jess. She is fourteen years old and knock kneed but a good worker. Jess had her colt with no difficulty and Bert called the lively little thing "Dandy". So Bert now has his six horses that he needs for the three furrow Imperial plough. He was able to turn over eight acres a day in the spring. Mind you, the day began at sun up and ended at sunset, ten hours a day in June, and he got the crop in by June 24, marked with big red letters on the calendar beside the stove.

During the long days Bert spent in the fields, Lynda and I were busy as well. Lynda is walking now, toddling around on her fat little legs. She is saying a few words, Mama of course being her first although Da was not far behind. She is fascinated with the cats, big old Wacko especially, and calls him by name. She tries, unsuccessfully, of course, to ride on his back. Luckily, Wacko is very good natured about it all, and runs off when it's too much for him.

Lynda follows me around as I do my daily tasks in the morning. Sometimes we bake pies or cookies, and Lynda helps roll out the dough or samples the fruit for the saskatoon pies. She also "helps" with dusting the furniture and sweeping the floors, although like her mother, she much prefers the baking to the house cleaning. In the afternoons, we go out to the garden and the barn. My garden on the sunny side of the house is beginning to grow well, although the weeds threaten to outgrow the vegetables as the summer heat increases. Lynda attempts to help me with the weeding but she's too young yet to recognize weeds, so I usually put her in a little patch of dirt on one side of the garden so she can make her own decisions about what lives and what dies. In the barn, we are allowed only a few tasks. Bert milks our three cows before going out to the fields, so I go out early every morning to run the separator and store the milk in our ice cellar. I churn butter out of the cream and store it there as well. Tomorrow Lynda and I will take both in to the creamery in the buggy.

Lynda and I collect the eggs from our twenty some hens whose nests line the barn wall. Sometimes we find eggs tucked away into odd corners in the straw on the floor under the nests. We also take the slop from the house to feed our three pigs. Looking after the horses and doing the field work is men's work in Bert's opinion. He has hired several men over the last few months to help him. Unfortunately, they have all been "green" Englishmen, fresh off the boat. They had no idea about farming and he had to let them go. I know that Bert is hoping for a son soon who will eventually be a help and an heir for him. I too hope for that, although I think that I and Lynda as she grows older could do much more to help if only Bert would allow it!

Some afternoons we go berry picking. I love the times we spend picking the saskatoons, chokecherries and currants that grow along the creek. Lynda and I take Wowser the dog with us, and after a few hours we usually pick enough to make jam. I have been able to can several quarts of saskatoons which will make great pies for desserts next winter. We will be able to taste summer then and perhaps banish from our minds for a short time the bitter winds that blow outside the door, sometimes making the snow drifts so high and hard that I cannot open the door without Bert's help. But why think or write about winter in the wonderful heat of summer?

Yesterday, Lynda and I had a good day even if it was slightly marred by yet another misadventure with the horses. When Bert left, I didn't pack him a lunch as we decided that Lynda and I would take lunch out to him in the far field. I prepared a special meal: freshly made bread, home cured ham, our own butter, a flask of tea and and some saskatoon tarts. I thought fondly of that special picnic day we had enjoyed when I first met and fell in love with Bert in Devon. I hoped that perhaps we could rekindle some oI the romantic feelings we had for each other then.

As we weren't going to town, I decided to take dear old Jess, the knock kneed mare, and let the colt run along beside us. I packed Lynda and the food into the buggy and we set out. I stopped along the way to pick some red currants that I spied, lush and ripe beside the path. I picked happily as Lynda sat nearby, playing with the cloth doll I'd recently made for her. When my bucket was full, we climbed back in the buggy and continued on to the field where Bert was working. Something was wrong. Jess kept veering into the hay stooks and stopping to eat. I couldn't seem to get her to stay on the trail. The colt of course followed his mother's lead, having a great time snacking along the way. Finally, as the sun grew hotter and hotter, we made it to where Bert was ploughing. He reined in his six horses with ease and came over to sit in the shade where I was putting down the blanket and laying out the food.

"Looks grand," said Bert, "but I expected you earlier."

"I've had an awful time with Jess since we stopped to pick currants."

Bert went over to investigate. "No wonder", he said, "the bit has slipped out of Jess's mouth! What fun for a quiet mare and colt to have an outing like this!" Then his tone became disapproving. "Nell, you have to be more careful, especially since Lynda is with you. You can't have any more runaways!"

I felt ashamed and a little humiliated but forced myself not to show these emotion. "How silly of me not to notice. It must have happened when I stopped by the creek to pick currants. Oh well, we are here now. Let's eat!"

Soon all three of us were enjoying the picnic. Bert and I both love ham, especially on freshly baked bread and eaten outdoors. The tea from the new flask I had recently bought at Mr. Dodd's store was still very hot and surprisingly thirst quenching. Bert was jovial and kept saying how happy he was to see us both, and we had a relaxing hour in the cool shade before Bert said "All good things must come to an end! Back to work!" He climbed on the plough and soon he was far up the field in a cloud of dust.

Lynda and I had a great trip home. Jess was easy to handle and trotted along as quickly as she could. Lynda laughed as the colt cavorted along side the buggy. I loved being out in the fields, away from the chores of house and garden! I felt happy and free and began singing an old song from my childhood. Lynda was able to join me with a few words. We sang loudly and off key; no one to hear us but the horses.

"Put on your old grey bonnet
with the red ribbons on it
And I'll hitch old Dobbin to the sleigh
Through the fields of clover
We'll ride on to Dover
On our golden wedding day!"

It was such a wonderful day. However, as I thought about it when I was about to fall asleep last night, I remembered Bert's tone of voice when he discovered why Jess was misbehaving. These thoughts put a cloud over the memories of the day. I realized that once again I'd been incompetent with the horses and although it wasn't as serious as the incident with Dolly, t still left me with an uneasy feeling which I couldn't shake. In the darkness of our bedroom, with Bert sleeping soundly beside me, these thoughts kept running through my mind in an endless circle of sadness.

November 10

Threshing season is over. How busy we've been! Bert started to cut the wheat on August 28th and threshing didn't finish until November 7th. It was a long, exhausting time, although somehow exhilarating as well. Luckily, Bert was able to hire a good man, John Goyne, to do the stooking* and drive the stook team. They worked from four in the morning until ten at night. Bert insisted on doing the chores when he got home, things I could easily help him with but he feels very strongly that my place is in the house.

The grain was all in stooks before Harvey Brown and his threshing crew arrived in October with the huge complicated machine which separates the grain from the chafe. Brown has a modern threshing machine and a crew of a dozen men as well as several teams of horses and wagons. The crew moves from farm to farm and have to work fast because of the possibility of weather change. Rain or even snow can mean crop failure and little money for farmers and threshers. They also need to move on to commitments at other farms. So they threshed what Bert had stooked and came back three different times before they had finished threshing the entire crop.

When the men chatted during meals, I heard many stories of tragic accidents due to fatigue. The machine is driven by steam and has all kinds of exposed belts and pulleys. These can be dangerous and can catch a piece of clothing, dragging a man into the machine, sometimes resulting in loss of fingers, hands, entire arms. Fortunately,

Harvey Brown runs a good crew and does not push his men to total exhaustion. I did not witness a tragedy this season, although I certainly witnessed stress and felt it many times myself.

Luckily for me, Bert hired Bertha Parker to help me feed that hungry crew of twelve men. She is a clever young woman, very competent in the kitchen and such a help to me as we prepared huge meals morning noon and night. Bert's brother Len has immigrated to Canada and is living with us now and helping with the threshing. He and Bertha seem to be enjoying each other's company. Hopeless romantic that I am, I would like to see sparks kindle between Bertha and Len. I like Bertha so much and Len reminds me of Bert when we first met, although not as handsome of course. His features are somehow courser and he isn't as slim but those blue eyes are the same! Bert keeps telling me that Len will be true to Eva Thorne, his girl in England, and I know I shouldn't hope for anything else. I am being unrealistic again, but I like the idea of reliving those early romantic times Bert and I had by watching Len and Bertha's possible romance blossom.

Back to reality though. The threshers certainly can eat! Bertha and I are happy to see them enjoying the food we put outside on long trestle tables. As the weather gets colder, they need more and more food to keep going. Before first light we serve bacon, eggs, potatoes and mounds of bread, butter and jam. The kerosene lanterns give a gloomy atmosphere to the meal but the men shovel everything we prepare into their mouths, fuel for the long day ahead. Around noon we carry huge baskets of sandwiches and flasks of tea down to the field beside the barn. The men stop only long enough to grab some food and a "cuppa", before Brown yells, "Everyone back to work! Lots to do before sunset." At the end of the day, the crew comes up to the house, exhausted and starving. Bertha and I work in the hot kitchen all afternoon preparing and cooking the supper. We have potatoes, corn on the cob, carrots, and beets out of the garden. We always cook a huge roast of beef or pork, sometimes ham. We serve the meal outside on a long trestle table. The flickering light of the kerosene lanterns gives just enough light as the sunset streaks the western sky. Although the men are dead tired and ready for their beds in the barn, they always revive enough to devour at least four pies: saskatoon, apple, or raisin, sometimes lemon meringue if we find ourselves with a little extra time in the kitchen.

As fall approaches, the men begin to realize that the end is in sight. They talk enthusiastically about the bumper crop, which means money for everyone. The crew is anxious to return to families and begin spending their hard earned cash.

Although the threshing had started poorly with three days of rain, once everything dried out, it went very well. We got 25 bushels to the acre, 2300 bushels in all, and Mr. Brown had enough wagon teams to haul the grain to the elevators.

"This crop will set us well on our feet" Bert said the night the threshing was finally finished. "We may now be in a position to realize our dream of buying our own farm. He talked cautiously though as he wanted to be very sure of our financial position before we settle on a place which will probably be our home for the rest of our lives.

Although we don't talk about the details, Bert no doubt feels that choosing the right farm is a man's responsibility. I think we share an underlying feeling that the right place will not only be a viable farm, but also a place where the land reaches out to us with a special voice. Bert often talks of the importance of water and I dream of a place with a creek running through it, a quiet sanctuary lined with trees, perhaps even a fairy ring like the magical place where Bert and I first fell in love.

There it is again. My hopeless romanticism gets in the way of logic. Perhaps Bert is right to be frustrated with me at times, although I do try to be practical and have become quite good at gardening, cooking, putting up preserves, and all the other tasks required of a farm wife. This leaves me little time for the sewing that I love, although I do find time to sew clothes for Lynda. She is thrilled that I am now working on a set of dresses for her special doll.

July 10, 1908

I am afraid I am not a good journal writer. I have plenty of time in the winter, but no inclination or enthusiasm for recording my thoughts. I am afraid I am not a winter person and the harshness of the climate here does not suit me. I often get the winter blues and I feel so physically tired that I question my ability to get through the days, especially when it gets dark at 4 pm and the long evening stretches in front of us. Fortunately, Bert and I are both readers. The few books we have are dog-eared. I must admit becoming too familiar with them and a bit bored with the plots. Bert alternates between reading the Farmers Weekly and Shakespeare. He brought his beloved copy of the complete works from England and never tires of rereading the plays. I would like to see a Shakespeare play performed some day. Reading the plays just doesn't appeal to me. The language is too difficult and perhaps my imagination lacks whatever it takes to make the action come alive.

We do go out occasionally. We bundle up Lynda and go off in the cutter, bells tingling and the stars bright in the winter sky. We visit Bill and Cecilia most often. Their new home is cozy and decorated in a way that reminds me of our house in Devon. Cissy, as everyone here calls her, is a great cook, and sets a lovely, very proper table: butter knives and bread and butter plates and cut glass goblets. Dessert and tea are served on a beautiful Royal Dalton English Rose tea set which she brought with her from England. Someday I hope to have some china: in fact, I know which set I love, Royal Albert Greenwood Tree.

Someday, someday.

We also visited with neighbours and they returned the visit and so the winter passed. The spring was very slow in coming. In fact, it snowed on the second of May. To make matters worse, this year after the crop was in, Bert decided that since Len was here to look after things, he would go out west with Ernie Goodlands to look at land. They went as far as Swift Current and hunted around for two weeks. They knew a Canadian veteran of the Boer War who had a section of land so were able to stay with him and his wife. Their friends were busy with their homestead duties; they had built a house and barn and had three years to show improvements to the land before it would belong to them. This opportunity was not available to Englishmen. Bert said he did look at some cheap land in the area, but he decided it was too remote; a long way from the railway, whereas at Melita, the railway is right in the town. We have three grain elevators and even a mill so that the flour we use comes from our own grain, As a daughter of a miller, this seems important to me.

Bert has come home, saying he had been lonely for us, and had decided that renting land was best for now. I am glad to have him home, although he was soon putting in long days as he and Len did the haying. Len has rented a farm for next year and his dearest Eva as he calls her will be coming from England soon.

My life has been made more interesting as we have bought two new horses; I love to see them in the fields! My favourite is a young bay colt which we have named Jumper because he runs and jumps like a deer. Bert is breaking him to ride and drive and he is proving to be an excellent saddle horse as well as being good at farm work.

We also have Jumper's brother, a chestnut coloured horse we have named Don. Unfortunately, Don is too spirited to use for farm work, but Bert has trained Jumper and Don to work as a team, first on the wagon and then on the sleigh. They are fast! It is very exciting to be be in the sleigh behind them when we go out visiting in the winter. I would love to learn to drive them but Bert said absolutely not. "Much too rambunctious for you, my darling!" I knew Bert will never forget my misadventures with Dolly. I waver between being thankful that he is thinking of my welfare and Lynda's too, and being resentful that he never gives me a chance to do anything remotely exciting!

Bert's practical approach to my handling the horses proved to be necessary. When the three of us went to church in Melita yesterday, we took the buggy with Don and Jumper as a lively and beautiful team. After church some of the parishioners came over to admire our horses. Many of our friends and neighbours think that possessing a good team is a necessity of life and of death as well. Mr Harris who runs the funeral home has a wonderful pair of black Arabians; they have fancy harnesses with black netting and the hearse itself has glass panels, with wheels that can be changed to runners, making it a sleigh in the winter time.

"What a spirited pair you have there, Bert. They look like they could give you quite a ride!" Mr. North said enthusiastically and the others who gathered around the buggy all agreed.

We said our good byes and were soon on the way home. Mr. North's comment about Don and Jumper's spirit proved all too accurate. As we were passing some bales of wire which our neighbour had set beside the road in readiness for building a fence, the horses spooked. They got into some wolf willow beside the road and then bolted into the plowed field. Bert managed to keep them in the field, but the furrows were very deep and the buggy bounced up and down, up and down. Bert realized he had to let the horses run and so we all hung on tight. Lynda had a wee umbrella and clung to it tightly the whole time. It took the better part of an hour, galloping across the furrows, before the horses tired and Bert was able to guide them back to the road. Bert said we were very lucky to have avoided a "crack-up" that is, the buggy tipping over. Because the buggy is so light, it's difficult to control a team once they get going at top speed. Bert says that he now feels very nervous about taking the buggy out with both horses.

November 16, 1908

Two more incidents with Don and Jumper. Many of my journal entries seem to be about the horses. Bert and I both love them so much. I sometimes think that I write about them to avoid thinking and writing about other matters, about how my feelings for Bert seem to be shifting somehow into a place which I don't want to acknowledge.

Two weeks ago we were in town shopping. Bert had let Lynda and I out on Main Street. At the bottom of Main, some dogs began barking loudly at the horses' heels. I saw the horses take off down Front Street, obviously out of control. I was horrified, but had to trust that Bert would be able to slow them down and return safely. I did my shopping as best I could and Lynda and I went to sit in the front booth of Happy's Chinese cafe so we could keep an eye on the street. Soon the buggy came into sight, the horses in a sweat and Bert looking somewhat disheveled. We quickly paid our bill at the counter and went out to climb in the buggy for the ride home. Bert said, "They ran for two miles, but I did manage to keep them on the road. Then they seemed to tire a little; I kept saying "whoa boys" until they finally slowed to a walk and I was able to turn them around. I was so relieved that the run away happened after you and Lynda got out."

Yesterday we were coming home from town with the sleigh. It was good sleighing but there were some drifts on the road. We were trotting along nicely when suddenly we hit a drift. Over we went! The seats were loose so we all fell out in a heap in the snow. Lynda screamed and burst into tears and I was very afraid. Bert managed to hold on to the reins but the team was frightened as well so they galloped off, dragging Bert with them. He realized he had to let them go. So we decided that Lynda and I would walk the half mile home and Bert would go after the horses. We left the cutter and most of the groceries in the drift. It was dark. Days are very short in November, but luckily there was a nearly full moon and the stars glittered on the snow.

We were dressed warmly and got home safely. The horses soon tired of galloping in the deep snow, so Bert brought them home about a half hour later.

We all went out this morning to gather up the rest of the groceries and to assess the damage to the cutter. Fortunately, the damages were quite minor and Bert says he will be able to fix it himself. He decided then and there that we will stick to single drivers and he will sell Don to Harry Ainsley, the horse trader. Jumper by himself is very steady and Bert feels comfortable about letting me drive the cutter and the buggy. I am so fond of driving and love the independence it gives me. My being able to go to town without him is a big help to Bert when he is busy on the farm.

September 6, 1909

Threshing time again and I'm too busy to write much, but I must record the exciting news. Lynda will soon have a little sister or brother which I know is Bert's preference, although he never says so in so many words. I am very tired most of the time and the doctor says I must take time to rest. Dr. Creighton is an old-fashioned doctor and would like to see all his pregnant patients in bed for the last few months. Of course, this is a completely unrealistic dream for me and most other farm wives. The baby is due at the end of December so hopefully when threshing is over I will have some time to rest.

February 2, 1910

Ground Hog Day. Overcast and a blizzard outside. of course the silly ground hog didn't see his shadow. Such a ridiculous North American notion anyway. Here on the prairies there is always six weeks more of winter!

I must not waste my energy writing about foolish things as I want to write about the most important event in my life since I wrote last fall, the birth of my darling Nora Mildred. Bert has nicknamed her his little maid, and I have started thinking of her as Maidie. Nora is my sister's name, and Mildred is Bert's sister. Somehow both of those names don't really suit her, so Maidie she will be.

What I record here will be mostly second hand information because I almost died after Maidie was born and drifted in and out of consciousness for days and days. These stories come from Bert and dear Miss Oxley and others who visited and cared for me during that dreadful time.

Nora Mildred made her appearance on Boxing Day. The birth went well; Dr Creighton and Miss Oxley were both at the house for the birth. Dr. Creighton left once he saw that mother and babe were doing well. Miss Oxley planned to stay to help until I was on my feet again. She has some training as a nurse and is becoming a dear friend to us; she is kind, compassionate, hard working and has a sadness about her. I have heard stories about her losing her fiancé during the Saskatchewan Rebellion. However, that story is for another time.

The day after Maidie was born, I was feeling well enough to eat some goose left over from Christmas dinner. By 5 o'clock I was sick and vomiting, almost unconscious. When Bert came in from chores, I heard Miss Oxley imploring Bert to get Dr. Creighton quickly. "Please Mr Townsend. I can't take the responsibility. Your wife is very ill." That's the last conversation I remember hearing so I have pieced together the story of those dreadful days from talking to Bert and Miss Oxley. Apparently, I was delirious, laughing, crying and talking too much. I kept sitting up in bed and trying to get up. My temperature was very high, my pulse racing. Bert went into Melita in the cutter to fetch Dr. Creighton. He was just going out to a Christmas party and wanted to put off seeing me for a few hours. Bert pleaded, saying that Miss Oxley believed it was urgent, even critical. Apparently, the doctor went off "in a huff" - Bert's words - but he got Jack Briggs with his team and cutter and they were at our place before Bert got home. Just as Bert rushed in, Dr. Creighton was slapping me sharply across the face to make me quiet down. I settled somewhat and he gave me sleeping tablets. He left Miss Oxley with some instructions and off he went to the party, saying he would return early in the morning.

Bert told me later that he felt his world was coming to an end; he was afraid I was dying and I understand now that indeed I was very close to death. Dr. Creighton explained when he returned the next morning that I had peritonitis. Inflammation had set in and that if I survived for ten days and gained some strength, he would operate to remove the inflamed part. He said "I'm afraid, Bert,

I have to be honest. I can't offer much hope yet for your wife's recovery."

I did gain consciousness sometimes. Every time I woke, Bert would be at my bedside holding my hand. I remember telling him I wanted to get better to look after Baby. However, my legs and feet were so swollen I couldn't get out of bed. To complicate matters, Miss Oxley had to leave for another job. Dr Creighton got in another nurse, Annie Craig. She was a very good nurse but she was young and not fond of children. For a few days, Nurse Griffins was here as well to look after the children. She was older and light hearted. She liked a nip of brandy at night and I would take a little as well. Bert says that it made me perk up a bit. I worried so much about the girls. Baby was not thriving. I was too sick to nurse her properly and she did not take well to cow's milk. Although I wanted to keep Lynda with me, at five she was very aware of the sadness around her. She was also visibly jealous of Baby. I saw her looking at me oddly when I was holding Maidie. Yesterday Maidie was asleep in her cradle. Nurse Griffins and Annie were both out of the room. Lynda was standing over the cradle. Suddenly, Maidie started to scream. Lynda stepped away quickly and Nurse Grieg came running, she picked up the baby and soon calmed her.

Lynda stood by my bed, her eyes lowered, whispering "Mommy, Baby cries all the time. I liked it better when you and I were here by ourselves." Lynda and I had spent so much time together that I could see she was finding it very hard to tolerate this new little creature who was so demanding of my time and attention. I realized then that Lynda had pinched or poked Baby. I also realized that until I was on my feet, I needed to listen to Bert's advice. He has been urging me to let Will and Cecilia take Lynda for a few days. I know this is the best plan; they will take good care of her. Cecelia is expecting a baby herself in a few months and will be thrilled to have Lynda until I am better.

So I hugged Lynda and whispered to her "You are going to stay with Uncle Will and Auntie Cissie for a little while You will have a grand time and your Dad will take you in the sleigh. Remember the jingle bells on the horse's harnesses that we put on for Christmas? You'll be able to listen to them as you go over the glistening snow."

"But Mommy, please let me stay with you! I promise to be good!" I could tell though that the jingle bells were appealing to her, so eventually I was able to convince her that the visit with Auntie and Uncle was a good idea after all.

February 28 1910

I was too tired to write more in my last entry, so now I want to continue the story of Maidie's birth and its aftermath.

After Lynda went to stay with Will and Cissie, I had a few days of rest. Baby Maid was seeming to be a little more content with her food, and Bert tried to keep up my spirits as he sat holding my hand in the evenings.

On the eleventh day, Dr. Creighton examined me and decided I was strong enough for the operation. In the afternoon, he brought another doctor to assist him with the anesthetic and the operation. Of course I remember nothing of the operation but when I awoke, I was very sore and somehow I knew then knew that the recovery would be quite long. In fact, I worried that this experience might affect my health for years, perhaps my whole life. I felt an overwhelming wave of depression. Would I ever have the strength to return to anything resembling a normal life?

I overheard Bert's conversation with the doctor. "It was a success, Bert, and I believe now that if we can get her eating, she will get better."

The last thing I felt like doing was eating. All I could seem to get down was jello, which Dr Creighton said had no food value but wouldn't hurt me. "Let her eat it, but try to get her eating some solid food," he told Bert. I couldn't stomach milk but Dr. Creighton prescribed Ergot of Rye to increase my appetite Gradually, I was able to take tea toast and soup.

Miss Oxley has a wealth of knowledge about all things medicinal, their traditions and history. She gave me a detailed account about the history of Ergot of Rye. Although Doctor had prescribed it as an appetite enhancer, apparently it also has properties which can reduce bleeding and is sometimes used to help expel the placenta and contract the uterus after childbirth. In medieval Europe, eating bread made with the ergot fungus caused the disease called St. Anthony's Fire; its hallucinogenic effects were so strong that many died. The disease has also been associated with the witch trials in Salem and in various places in Europe. The women convicted and sometimes killed as witches suffered from some of the same symptoms as those who suffered from ergot poisoning: vomiting, vertigo, the sensation of things crawling on the skin, hallucinations.

"Isn't it amazing," Miss Oxley said, "that the same ergot that once caused such damage has been harnessed by modern medicine to good effect."

What was amazing for me was Miss Oxley herself. We were happy that she was able to return to us, and that we could have Lynda back at home. Unfortunately, Baby Maid was still not thriving. Miss Oxley said right away "Why, this baby hasn't been looked after properly since I left. How could a baby thrive with a mouth like this? It's a white mouth, a yeast infection which is quite common in babies. It's passed from the breast milk to the dear little one, but I know just what to do to cure it. I'll get some baby food at Dodd's store to mix with the milk and in no time Babe will be better. True to her word, in three weeks Baby Maid was, in Miss Oxley's words, "the sweetest, cutest, and happiest baby one could wish for."

Miss Oxley was so wonderful at caring for me and the children. She worked long hours yet was able to keep up her good spirits. Bert kept telling her that having her in the house was a godsend. She and Bert took turns rubbing blue stone on the flesh wound where my operation had been. Miss Oxley told me the amazing history of the blue stone she carries with her always. It is very precious because it came from Stonehenge and because the healing properties of this stone are well known by women everywhere who have inherited the knowledge of the ages. Blue is a cooling colour and therefore the stone is particularly effective in treating inflammation. Bluestone is also associated with communication and Miss Oxley whispered to me once when Bert was out of hearing: "This crystal is also powerful in helping with affairs of the heart. It will improve your marriage!" If only that will prove to be true!

Nevertheless, I was extremely slow to heal and I was so weak. I weighed only eighty pounds and Bert could pick me up easily. He sometimes carried me from my bed to the rocking chair by the window where I would sit, wrapped in a quilt, Lynda playing on the floor nearby and Baby peacefully asleep in her cradle. From my window vantage point I could see the barn and sometimes the horses as Bert fed them. It was seeing my darling children and my beloved horses that made me realize that I would recover, that death was not going to get me this time. I gradually began to gain a little strength.

Miss Oxley kept telling me that I was very fortunate to have had Dr. Creighton, "a very clever man", she said. "In my experience, not many women recover from peritonitis." She herself had had the sad experience of seeing new mothers in her care die. She told me that historically even more women ended their lives in the aftermath of child birth, dying of the dreaded inflammation and its accompanying fever. She told me that not all of Henry VIII's wives had been beheaded like poor Anne Boleyn; both Jane Seymour and Catherine Parr had died from peritonitis.

Unfortunately, Miss Oxley had to leave to go to another case after six weeks. I miss her so much: her compassion, her interesting stories, her companionship. Talking to her, I feel part of a sisterhood of women, strong and independent, who can do important things in the world. Miss Oxley is not young, in her mid forties, I would estimate. Like me, she does not discuss her age. She has shared with me the story of why she never married. She told me that she was very much in love as a young girl and was engaged, unofficially, she said, as they had not told their families of their plans to marry. Andrew was a hired man on a farm outside Melita and was considered by her parents to be unsuitable. They met secretly, often sneaking off to be together after a long day of work, telling their parents that they had to work late. Miss Oxley's face grew animated when she told me about that happy time. I can imagine how beautiful she must have been as a young girl! Of course, she didn't share all the details of those secret meetings but I know we were both thinking of similar things, of romance in the prairie grasses!

Then in 1885, Colonel Middleton's troops came west from Ontario on the newly built CPR to fight Louis Riel and his rebels. Andrew went to Virden and met the train. Like many hundreds of young men from the west, he joined the troops, more for the adventure he said, than for any political or nationalistic motives. In fact, he told Miss

Oxley that from what he'd heard, Riel was an interesting character, a visionary who should be credited rather than blamed for his part in the Red River Rebellion of 1870, which after all, resulted in the creation of Manitoba as a province. Given his feelings about Riel, it is indeed ironic that Andrew was one of the eight of Middleton's men who were lost at the Battle of Batoche, shot down by rebel fire. Miss Oxley had tears in her eyes and her voice was low and sad as she told me this story, even though many years have passed since his death. I held her hand as she told me that she her heart was truly broken and that she never even looked at another man. I often think of Andrew and of Riel, who was hanged as a traitor in Regina after the rebellion. I have always been fascinated by what I've read and heard about Riel. Bert calls him a traitor and a dirty Metis and I keep my silence. I know in my heart that Andrew's assessment of him is closer to the truth. Perhaps someday his place in the history of the west will be recognized as a positive one. *

Luckily, Bert was able to find a girl named Ethel Horner to come to live here and look after the children and to do the cooking and cleaning. Of course she is not a trained nurse but she is competent and friendly. She will be able to stay as long as we need her.

So gradually I am recovering and am able to get up for an hour or two a day. I often eat a late supper with Bert after Ethel has tucked the babes into their beds and retired to her room. We have had some long and very heart warming conversations. One topic on both our minds, of course is buying our own farm. Bert had been negotiating with a Mr. Cameron to rent another farm, but my illness has made the move impossible, He has cancelled the arrangement and we have leased this place for two more years. I am quite happy here and Bert is too. I am looking forward to the spring and summer, and to getting strong enough to care for Maid and Lynda. I hope I will be strong enough to plant a large garden and to go berry picking, two of my favourite summertime activities. I can already feel the sunshine on my face! When I think of cooking, canning, and feeding the threshing crews come August, I am a little unsure of my capabilities. Will I recover enough strength to be a good farm wife and a caring partner in our marriage? Bert has been so very kind and loving throughout this entire ordeal. I try to suppress my nagging doubts about the solidness of our relationship. As we sat together last evening, some of the old romantic feelings were definitely there. I hope we will be able to sustain them when I return to good health.

Riel is now acknowledged as the founder of Manitoba. Louis Riel Day is celebrated the third Monday in February as a provincial statutory holiday.

March 13, 1912

A year has gone by since I last found the time or inclination to write. With the winds of March blowing wildly outside, we are all in the kitchen, cozy by the stove and I have time to write for awhile. Lynda and Maid are already in bed. The darkness comes early enough that they are content to go willingly to their warm beds. Lynda has reached the stage where she is no longer jealous and she loves to cuddle the baby, as we all do. I feel so blessed to be alive and surrounded by my loving family. Bert is reading his Shakespeare as he so often does. Perhaps he is reading about Julius Caesar and the Ides of March, a special day for us as it is Bert's birthday. I am already planning a special meal, with an angel food cake as dessert. We will have candles. The girls will love that! We are on own now with no help, as I am "just about" well, as Bert keeps saying.

Last fall's crop was a bumper one and the big threshing gang was kept very busy. I was still too tired to do very much but we had an extra girl to help Ethel. Her name is Lizzie Stainsthorpe, and she is young, blond and lively. She is very pretty with white skin, big blue eyes, and her sunny disposition matches her looks. I sometimes noticed Bert looking at her for what seemed like a long time. Once I looked out the window and observed Bert and Lizzie involved in what appeared to be a very earnest conversation in the shade of the barn. I felt pangs of jealousy but I told myself I was being foolish. Soon Lizzie came skipping into the kitchen with the eggs she'd gone to collect and we got busy preparing a meal for the threshing crew. I tried to push my jealous feelings to the back of my mind and Lizzie and I got along well for the rest of the time she was with us. However, I still have nagging doubts about her. Bert always seemed so animated when she was nearby.

Bert was very happy with our crop: more wheat than all our neighbours. "It's an act of Providence, our grand crop" he told me when the threshing was done and we had money in the bank. Cameron's farm, which we had almost rented last year was hailed out completely so my illness after Maidie's birth had one positive effect on us. If we had moved as planned, our finances would be in very poor shape. "It's an ill wind that blows no good," Bert has said more than once this winter.

We have begun to talk about a trip home to England now our financial position is more secure. We both realize that this trip will probably postpone our dream of owning our own farm. However, we want to see our families and have our parents spend some time with their Canadian grand daughters, as they refer to them in their letters. We are planning to go next winter and we will be away four months. Bert is already looking into the travel arrangements and searching for a responsible man to look after the farm while we are gone.

I have finally come to the last page of the journal I began at the beginning of my life in Canada. I will place it at the very back of my canning shelves in the basement, a place where Bert is unlikely to find it.

Journal Three

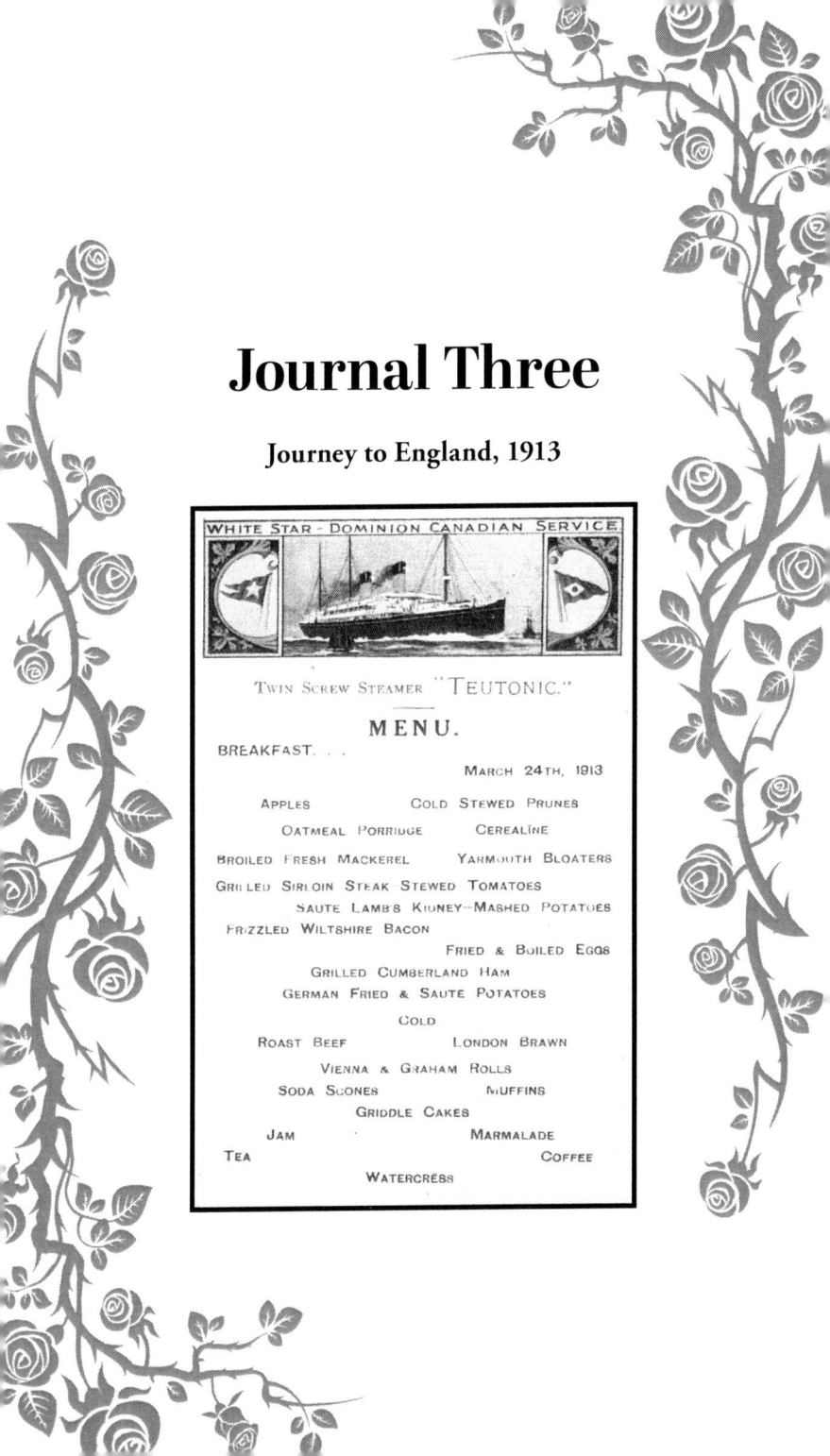

Journey to England, 1913

WHITE STAR - DOMINION CANADIAN SERVICE

Twin Screw Steamer "Teutonic."

MENU.

BREAKFAST...

March 24th, 1913

Apples   Cold Stewed Prunes
Oatmeal Porridge   Cerealine
Broiled Fresh Mackerel   Yarmouth Bloaters
Grilled Sirloin Steak Stewed Tomatoes
Saute Lamb's Kidney—Mashed Potatoes
Frizzled Wiltshire Bacon
Fried & Boiled Eggs
Grilled Cumberland Ham
German Fried & Saute Potatoes

Cold

Roast Beef   London Brawn
Vienna & Graham Rolls
Soda Scones   Muffins
Griddle Cakes
Jam   Marmalade
Tea   Coffee
Watercress

Gillingham, January 4, 1913

I have brought my new journal, a small, thick hard covered note book with a red cover I bought at the store in Melita. However, I was much too sick during the crossing to write, eat, or indeed do anything but lie in my berth. Bert and the girls were fine. They got their "sea legs", Bert said, and thoroughly enjoyed the journey. I think I was already exhausted before we boarded the ship as we had to make the long journey to Portland, Maine by train. We found travelling with the children quite a change from our memories of travel when we emigrated. The noise of the train itself, the constant conversations with fellow travellers, the bustle of the cities we stopped in, were in sharp contrast to our quiet farm life. Lynda and Maidie enjoyed the excitement some of the time; at other times of course they were fussy and cried often, homesick as we were for familiar surroundings. When we we finally boarded the S.S Teutonic for Liverpool, I was relieved, even though I knew from my first trans Atlantic journey thatI was not a sailor.

We were on board for Christmas and Bert described the fine meal which was served: goose, duck, trifle, chocolates. His description went on and on. I had to shut my eyes and hope that the mere mention of food would not make me vomit all over the plaid coverlet on my berth. I tried to put on a brave face for Bert and the girls. "I'm so glad you and the girls enjoyed the fine meals".

Bert also described the luxurious surroundings in the dining room: crystal chandeliers, white linen table clothes, festive red and green table centres with candles that cast a magic glow over all. Alas, I never even got to set foot in that room. In fact, Bert had to carry me off the boat. After landing, I was ravenous and we stopped in a little place not far from the dock in Liverpool, where I stuffed myself with bread and jam. Bert joked with me, saying "Nell, we were on the boat for two weeks with all those grand meals already paid for, and now your appetite comes back!" Somehow, my face must have shown that I found his remark quite callous and unfeeling. I had been so sick. Didn't he realize that? He quickly took my hand: "My Darling, I am happy to see you hungry and feeling well so soon!" The girls also were happy and chatty, taking turns climbing into my lap and sharing bites of my bread and jam.

We travelled to London by train, and then down to Gillingham, a short journey compared to our train ride in North America! England looks like a garden, so fresh and green and tidy. We talked a lot about how it was so different from Melita and the farm; Canada is so big and rough somehow, and of course at this time of year, buried in feet of snow.

When we arrived in Gillingham, the bells were ringing the old year out and the new year in. It's almost unbelievable to be back at Waterloo Mill, not much changed from when I left. My parents are both well and delighted to have us here. They are making a great fuss over their Canadian grand daughters as they call them. Maid and Lynda are basking in all the attention. Of course, there have been many changes in my family. My youngest sisters, Nora and Beattie, are still living at home: in fact, Beattie is thinking of returning to Canada with us. She says she needs an adventure in her life! My brother Hubert has married and runs a small milk farm nearby. He says he plans to drive us around to "see the sights" soon. We also plan to go to London to visit my sisters Jane and Mary and their families. Of course, we are also going to Somerset to spend time with Bert's family. I am afraid Bert and I have already had some near-angry words about when exactly we should leave here. Now that I am here I would like to stay as long as possible. After all, we do have four months, but Bert is understandably anxious to see his family. he wants to leave here next week, and then come back to Gillingham later. So no doubt that's what we will do. Even here he is the one who makes the decisions. I am determined to make the most of this first visit and I am happy to know we will return soon for a longer stay. I must stop writing and go down to visit with Mother and Father. I know that once we buy a farm of our own in Manitoba, circumstances, financial and otherwise, will prevent us from making another trip across the ocean for a long, long time.

March 4, 1913 Watchet, Somerset

We have only a few days left in England. We sail on March 15, the Ides of March, Bert's birthday. I am so sad and exhausted by the events of the last two months that I am not sure that I will be able to write about them. Already my hand is shaking and tears are staining the page, blurring the ink, creating a rivulet of dark blue down the page. I think that recording my thoughts here might help me control the anger and the grief which keeps welling up inside of me.

I have blotted the rivulet of ink, controlled my shaking hand, and allowed myself to think back to when I was safe at home in Waterloo Mill with my family around me. I was enjoying my time with Mother and Father and the rest. Sister Beattie and I were having long conversations about her coming back to Canada with us. I told her all I could about the prairies and our life on the farm. She realizes that life with us would be a complete contrast to what she's used to. She has not done much travelling, only to London to visit family. I know she met someone there with whom she corresponds although she hasn't told me much about him. I kept encouraging her to book her passage so she could travel back with us. She finally decided to do so. "This will be good for me. I need some new experiences!" she told me. The thought of her company on the long return journey is the only a ray of sunshine for me among all the sad dark clouds which fill my mind.

I am still so upset with Bert that I can barely look at him and we have exchanged only brief meaningless words since we received the news about Mother.

But I must explain. Bert insisted that we leave Gillingham and go to his home in Somerset. Actually, Harwood Farm, which had been in the family since 1825. was in the process of being sold, so we divided our time between Watchet, where Bert's Mother lives with his sister Beat, and the Forester Hotel in Dunster. It is run by his brother John and wife Elsie who moved from the farm a few months ago. Bert is understandably upset that the farm will be no longer be in the family; he kept saying "the end of the yeoman family of Townsends at East Harwood". He and John went down there to shoot rabbits as they had in their childhood, and Bert was very nostalgic about it all. I took the girls down there one afternoon and as we stood looking over the fields, a view of the ocean in the distance, Bert broached the subject of our staying here, perhaps renting or purchasing part of the farm. "I would sooner have my Canadian home" I said. He looked away quickly and strode across the field to join John and to shoot more rabbits.

Elsie arranged a party and dance in honour of our visit in the hotel dining room. There were about thirty guests, family and close friends. After a great meal, the tables were pushed against the wall and four local musicians began to play lively music. We were all dancing; Lynda and Maid were in Bert's arms whirling around the floor, screaming in delight. It was such a jolly time! Alas, we had been dancing for only a short time when a hush fell over the room. A man I didn't recognize had come to the side door of the dining hall and whispered something to Elsie and John. They asked the musicians to stop playing and walked over to Bert. I couldn't quite hear what was being said, but I heard the words Waterloo Mill and knew then that it must be news from my home. Bert came over, took my hands and said: "My darling, there is no easy way to say this. Your mother has died." I heard no more. I fainted.

Of course we went back to Gillingham immediately. The funeral was a blur, although I was happy that Will and Cecelia were there as they too were in England that winter. Will was with Mother when she died. She had caught a cold which turned to pneumonia and she was gone within ten days. Will told me that they had sent word to Dunster that she was ill, but that Bert had decided not to tell me as he knew that I would want to return home, which would mean our leaving his family. My anger toward Bert is almost uncontrollable! Of course, he had no way of knowing how grave the situation was, but still I cannot forgive him. I am not sure I can ever forgive him. To be so close and to be denied the last few days with my dear Mother.

After the funeral, we stayed a few days at Waterloo Mill, but I was too overcome with grief to visit. My brother Hubert drove us around to see some beautiful sights: Stonehenge, Salisbury Cathedral, Bath. My heart was not in it. I tried to keep up my spirits, especially in front of the children, but tears came easily and I was so tired that I went off to my bed early, usually to near sleepless nights. We are now in Watchet with Bert's mother. Tomorrow we travel to London to visit with my bother Charley and my two married sisters there. Of course I saw them all at the funeral but it will be nice to visit their homes. I hope I can be happy in their company. Then it is on to Liverpool by train to board the boat for Canada. How will I endure the ocean voyage? The train journey? My overwhelming grief? My anger towards Bert?

Writing this seems to have intensified my grief and anger rather than alleviate those feelings. What will become of our marriage? Right now I feel such despair and loathing. I must end now. Bert stirs in the bed as I sit here at the small desk in our bedroom, writing long into the night. We of course have been sharing beds on our travels, but we both shrink as small as possible, careful not to touch each other.

I will get climb into bed now, slip under the covers very quietly and hope for a little sleep.

October 17, 1913 Melita, Manitoba

Months now since that horrible, horrible voyage home from England. I was still exhausted with grief when we boarded at Liverpool and of course I was seasick the whole way home. The crossing was so rough that almost everyone, except Bert, of course, was seasick. He was the only one at breakfast at our table some mornings. The seas were so rough that that the waves washed right over the decks and they had to "fasten the hatches" which meant they shut us down below for hours at a time. Two brothers from Melita, Bill and Cecil Parham, were also on the boat. Cecil nearly died when he went up on deck early one morning before the hatches were closed. He was so sick and disoriented that he came very close to being washed overboard. At the last moment he saved himself by grabbing the deck chairs, which were fastened to the floor.

Maidie was also very sick. The doctor said she got indigestion from eating too much cheese at one of their first meals on board, before the voyage turned into a nightmare of rolling seas and vomit everywhere. Luckily, Maid recovered fairly quickly, but sister Beattie and I were sick for the entire ten days. Then we still had to face the long rail journey home from Maine across half a continent. It is all a blur to me. We slept a lot, except Bert of course, who spent a lot of time visiting with fellow passengers, many of them new immigrants eager to hear his stories about farming on the prairies, which of course was what they planned to do once they got to their various destinations.

We were very relieved to see Melita's grain elevators on the horizon. In spite of all the sleep, we were still exhausted when we got off the train at the station, happy to see Len there with Jumper and the buggy to take us home. The girls were excited to see their own beds, and we soon had Beattie settled in the tiny spare room off the kitchen.

Bert has thrown himself into fall work and we talk very little. I despaired of ever being able to recover from the tragedy of my mother's death, but then....

Journal Four

A Farm of Our Own, 1913-1926

November 12, 1913

THE BIG EVENT:

IT HAS FINALLY HAPPENED – WE HAVE A FARM OF OUR OWN!

We won't actually be moving until spring, but Bert made the cash payment yesterday:

160 acres with a large barn, a small but very adequate house, and two granaries. The farm is right on the outskirts of town, near to school for the girls. A creek runs close to the buildings, so there will be plenty of water summer and winter. The cash payment was $2000, the remaining $5000 to be paid at 6%. Bert says we can handle the payments as the land is fertile, good crops ensured for years to come!

NW 1-4-27 will become our new home. Hopefully we will not have to move again so a long time, perhaps even our life times.

Bert had heard about a farm for sale one afternoon when he was having a scotch with Billy Cobb in the Met Hotel. The farm is close to town. Billy said they could walk to it in ten minutes and have a look, which they did. Bert came home in a state of tremendous excitement and asked me to come and look at the place before he made the final decision.

We went the very next day and I fell in love with the farm right away. Even in November, with a skiff of snow on the ground and hoar frost on the trees, it was beautiful. We walked along the creek with the girls: saskatoon and chokecherry bushes, a big elm tree with sheltering branches, and yes, a little open glen which reminded me so much of the fairy ring in Devon where we had the picnic and where I fell in love with Bert. He took my hand as we stood in the clearing, and for the first time since our trip to England, I thought that perhaps we could begin to work past the huge rift that had come between us over my mother's death.

Bert whispered to me: "This is a magic place! We will be happy here!"

We took the girls' hands and the four of us danced around the fairy ring.

April 3, 1914 Our New Home

April 1st was possession day. Beattie and I loaded the buggy with the girls and our three cats and we drove the few miles to the new farm. Jumper was lively and we were all so excited. Bert and the hired man had already moved the six work horses, the milk cows, and all our furniture, taking several trips in the wagon. Some neighbours helped and the move went quite quickly,

Getting settled in the house was a huge job but we were so energized by our dream come true that the time flew by. We worked all day, unpacking, setting up the kitchen, moving furniture, making up the beds. The house is more spacious than our rented one, with an attached shed where we have set up the cream separator. The kitchen is small, but we have the luxury of an indoor pump and the water runs clear and cold from it. The window in the kitchen looks out on the back yard; the large maple tree there has a great branch just crying out for a swing. I must get Bert to make one soon. I can already picture Lynda pushing Maidie, who is laughing with delight. There is a cleared area for a garden at the back as well and I am already imagining yellow daisies and baby's breathe and of course vegetables: leafy green lettuce, tomatoes ripening on the vine, the glowing colours of rainbow Swiss chard.

The wood stove in the corner of the large dining room is a modern one, a McClary with a warming oven and a reservoir for hot water! I am so looking forward to baking in it and preparing some great meals for us all. The house has two bedrooms on the main floor, a large one for Bert and me and smaller one for the girls. There are two tiny rooms under the eaves, up a very steep staircase with a nasty turn to it, but when the girls get bigger I think they will love the privacy up there. And of course, there is room for more children although Dr. Creighton has warned me of the dangers of another pregnancy. too much strain on my heart, he says. I know Bert longs for a son. We shall see....

For now, sister Beattie is happily settling into the upstairs room at the back, looking down on our garden to be. On the main floor, we have a screened verandah along the front which will be wonderful in the heat of summer. The main floor also has a sitting room where we have already put the settee we bought recently, our only piece of good furniture. I dream of a piano there some day, and a fern stand full of greenery, perhaps my favorite asparagus fern similar to the one in the sitting room at Waterloo Mill. How my mother loved that plant! Tears still come to my eyes every time I think of dear Mother, but I try to concentrate on the present and on making this house a proper home for Bert and the girls.

The house looks rather sparsely furnished right now, but we will gradually add new and special things to make it a real home. I want a good wooden table and a side board for the china I hope to have some day. I dream of comfortable chairs and a daybed for the verandah. This winter I will be busy sewing and knitting: curtains, pillow covers, a red afghan for the settee. My mind races ahead to how beautiful this place will be!

On moving day, when we finally sat down to a cup of tea at about 11 at night, we were exhausted but happy. "The only problem," I told Bert, "is that there are literally hundreds of mice scurrying everywhere. Our cats have already caught so many, but still they keep appearing!" As I spoke, a mouse ran under our feet, and Wacko, our most experienced mouser, did her best, but it somehow escaped through a tiny opening by the shed door.

Bert explained patiently: "Nell, I'm sorry to tell you this, but grain was been stored under the shed attached to the house and the mice have moved in and multiplied. The only way to eradicate them is to raise the floor of the shed and clean out all the grain. I plan to do that as soon as possible. We will also need put in a cement foundation, so it will be quite a big job. My darling, you'll have to put up with the mice for a few days."

"Luckily, I'm not the kind of woman who jumps up on a chair every time I see a mouse. Even a multitude of mice can't erase my joy at being in our own house on our own farm. What we've always dreamed of!"

To celebrate the occasion of our moving to our own farm, Bert bought me a very special gift. He and I have both become fascinated with the birds of the prairie, so different from the birds we remember from our childhoods in England. We of course know the names of the common ones: robins, meadowlarks, mourning doves. Often we often see birds which we cannot name.

The Secret Journals of Nell Clarke

So I was delighted when Bert presented me with a beautiful little book last week. It has a leather cover with a gold embossed bird and the title "Land Birds: Bird Guide, Song and Insectivorous Birds East of the Rockies." The title page inside includes an even longer title as the intriguing phrase "From Parrots to Bluebirds" is included along with the author's name Chester A. Reed. Bert ordered it by mail directly from the publisher, Musson Book Company in Toronto. He had seen it advertised in the Farmer's Weekly paper he subscribes to. He says that Reed, although still in his twenties, is the best known Ornithologist in North America and that this book is the first of its kind: small enough be carried easily and full of beautifully detailed coloured illustrations. I love the text as well because Reed writes so enthusiastically about each bird and in the preface describes how we need to protect birds, encourage them around our homes, and learn all we can about them by studying their habits and appreciating their beauty. I had always felt a little guilty about sitting quietly out in the garden, watching birds, but this book has made me realize that knowing birds is important to understanding our place in the world. Already we have used the illustrations to identify some of the many birds that live near the house, out in the fields, and in the wooded area around the creek. Perhaps the most interesting one so far is the Whip-Poor-Will, with its long bristles at the base of its bill and its barred wings. As we sat out in the yard at dusk last night, we saw one swooping down to catch a large moth. The book says that the female lays beautiful mottled coloured eggs of white, grey and lilac in a ground nest. Of course it has a very distinctive song: a whistled repetition of the sound has become its name. I wish I were better at recognizing bird song; Bert can hear a bird song once and then identify the bird by its song the next time he hears it. The whip-poor- will's sound is so unique, though, that even I will recognize it.

We also have a few species of hummingbirds, only one of which, the ruby throated, we've been able to identify so far. I love Reed's description of its nest: "a most beautiful creation of plant fibres and cobwebs adorned with lichens and resembling a little tuft of moss upon the bough on which it is placed." Perhaps I will see this tiny nest someday now I know what to look for. There are so many small birds in the guide, especially sparrows and warblers, that sorting them out will take some time. Reed says at the back of the guide that some bird watchers use field glasses to identify birds, and they can be ordered for $5.00. Bert says perhaps we can purchase some but I'm not sure I want to do that. It might spoil the magic!

I am so thrilled with this present to mark the special occasion of moving into our new home. I'm sure it will give us both hours of pleasure. I have been leafing through it as I write this and am so amazed at the beauty of both the writing and the illustrations. The book also lists other titles by the same author: flower and mushroom guides, books about water birds, and a bird book for children. There's even one about birds' eggs. Each book costs about $2.00 with 25 cents for postage so perhaps we will be able to order more books written by this amazing author.

February 28th, 1915

Almost a year since I wrote so happily on our moving day; our first year on the new farm has indeed been a magical time. Bert calls it "our little love nest" and the two of us are getting on very well, partly because I have felt better than I have since Maid was born. I am strong, healthy, and optimistic about the future. I got pregnant last fall, and was well the whole time. Bert and I both talked of the new baby and planned to call him Kenneth. I too would have liked a son, but we were both ecstatic when tiny Kathleen Audrey came to Valley Farm on the day after Valentine's Day, early on a Sunday morning.

Dr. Byers has replaced Dr. Creighton, who moved to Brandon, and he is gentle and kind. He came a few hours before the birth and was quietly competent. He seemed happy to let Miss Oxley handle most things, recognizing her experience at being a midwife. My labour was short, and I was soon sitting up in bed, nursing Babe and watching the sun rise through our bedroom window. What a contrast to Maid's birth, when I came so close to dying that I remember little of her entrance into this world.

Beattie is here to help with the girls and dear Miss Oxley has been able to stay with us for a few weeks. I will miss her so much when she goes next week. I love our conversations. We cover everything from news of the war in Europe and the Russian Revolution to child care and matters of the heart. She is indeed a "gem" as Bert says. She is caring and knowledgeable about so many things. I feel sad that she never married after her lover was killed in the North West Rebellion. However, she assures me that her life is full and satisfying, although she admits that sometimes as she cares for other women's babies, she wishes that she had been able to experience childbirth and the joy of motherhood.

She and I are both fascinated as we watch Lynda and Maidie with the new babe. Lynda is quite the little mother and is very fond of cuddling the baby. Maidie sometimes slips into our bedroom for a peek, but Lynda is right in there after her.

"You are much too young to hold her yet." Lynda tells her sternly.

Maidie pouts and comes running back to me and Miss Oxley with tears in her eyes. Then Miss Oxley will sometimes fetch Kathleen out of her bassinet, bring her into the kitchen close to the warm stove, and we take turns holding the baby. We all smile and enjoy her delicate beauty. Miss Oxley claims to have powers to see into the future of babies that she helps to birth, and predicts that Kathleen will be the creative one in the family: an artist, a musician, and a dreamer.

Of course, Miss Oxley was not present when Lynda was born, and because I was so ill with Maidie, no predictions were made at those births. We have been having interesting conversations now about Lynda and Maidie. They are both very dear to me and my ideas about how they are developing is perhaps clouded by my maternal instincts. It is wonderful to have Miss Oxley here to chat about their distinct personalities. She is such a clear thinker and I value her opinions. Lynda is ten now and has already been at school for four years. How the time flies by! Miss Oxley says Lynda is the strong practical one and I know that is true. Maidie will be trudging up the hill to school this fall, and I am thankful that she will have Lynda to go with her. Maidie is not as strong as Lynda although she is persistent and stubborn at times as well. Miss Oxley says Maidie is a combination of the creative and the practical; she will not be a dreamer like Kay, and she will be extremely clever and athletic. She will win prizes at school and be an amazing achiever. Lynda, on the other hand, is a "plodder" at school; her teachers say she does well, but it takes a lot of time and work on her part. They have both been such good children, not difficult at all. I was sincere when I told Bert that girls are much easier than boys and that I wasn't too disappointed that Kathleen was not the Kenneth we had hoped for.

I feel a little guilty that I have not recorded the girls' progress in more detail in my journals, although I do have a small trunk full of mementoes: locks of hair from their first hair cuts, baby clothes I have made, a few photos and a few notes about their first steps, their first words, their pets, their favourite toys, their special books. The girls are so central to my life, yet because things have gone so smoothly, I have not felt the necessity to write in great detail in my journal about them.

Instead, I have perhaps been preoccupied with horses and gardens and crops and of course always my relationship with Bert, whom I love so deeply. We are almost like newly weds right now. I pray that it will stay that way. I discuss this with Miss Oxley as well and she advises against the jealous feelings I often feel about him and other women.

She has told me often "He's good man, Nell, and he really cares for you. I have seen it over and over again, especially when you were near death when Maidie was born. Treasure that always."

May 15, 1916

I am bed ridden now with much time to contemplate my life and to write, but my depression and sadness interferes with my desire and ability to put into words what has happened in the last six weeks.

After Kay was born I felt so happy and robust. I thought that my poor health was a thing of the past and that I would have the energy to be a good wife and mother. And for awhile that was the case. 1915 was a good crop year, the best crop we had ever had. Our beautiful wheat harvested out at fifty and sixty bushels to the acre and at 75 cents a bushel. The war in Europe is good for farmers, Bert keeps saying, and the price of grain will to go up as long as the war continues. The news of the slaughter in the trenches seems to make the money making aspect of it all seem very uncivilized somehow. I worry that Bert might enlist; he sometimes talks nostalgically about his time in the Boer War, fighting for England. Fortunately, because Bert is a farmer and is married with children, he will not be drafted, at least not now. I pray that his patriotic ideals will remain thoughts and not actions.

It has been so wonderful having sister Beattie here with us. She and I were never close as children because of our age difference. Six years is a big difference when you are young, but now she has been a good companion to me and such a help with the children. She is naturally shy and coming to Canada with us was a very adventurous journey for her to undertake. Bert keeps hoping she will "pair up" with one of the hired men, but I know that is not going to happen. She has confided in me that farm life is much too "rough and ready" for her and she is homesick for England. She writes regularly to the man she met in London before she came to Canada. She is quite closed mouthed about the relationship. All I know is that his name is Sam and he is a bobby - a city policeman - quite handsome in his uniform in the photograph Beattie keeps by her bed. She plans to make the long journey back to England soon. I will miss her, but I know that this life isn't for everyone and I understand that she often thinks of Father, her siblings and of course, Sam. Understandably, she also longs for the gentle green hills of Devon and its milder climate.

Kay has been a good baby. Lynda and Maidie are both in school, happy and doing well. I did have to visit the school once when little Maidie came home in tears, saying that her left hand was being tied behind her back so that she would learn to hold her pencil and to print with her right hand. When she began to use her hands as a toddler, I noticed that she was extremely left handed, left sided in fact, but I saw no need to interfere. When she began to learn to write her letters at home, she always held the pencil with her left hand. Surely our inclinations are natural and should be left to develop as they will. The prejudices against left handedness originated in medieval time when myths of the left hand were associated with evil. I discussed this at length with Miss Oxley and she agreed, saying that in her experience with toddlers, it is important to allow the natural tendencies to develop in this matter. Otherwise there can be emotional damage to the child. At any rate, Maidie was visibly upset and sick to her stomach during the first few weeks of school.

One morning, when I was taking the horse and buggy to town, I dropped by the school to talk with Miss Bullock, the primary teacher. I told her that she had to stop this barbaric and out-dated method, and that under no circumstance was she to tie Maidie's left hand behind her back ever again. She was shocked at my straight forward and abrupt words and began to argue that in normal school they had been taught that this was a necessary procedure. I refuse to listen and left quickly, repeating my ultimatum. I was obviously persuasive because it has not happened since. Maidie loves school and is doing so well, proving that Miss Oxley's prediction for her is true. She is clever and quick in beginning to read and write.

That incident reminds me of how well I felt last fall. But in late March, I contracted measles and have been bedridden for weeks, an unusually serious case, the doctor says. Baby Kay got them too, although she recovered quite quickly, and by some miracle Bert and the girls did not get them.

I began to cough up blood and Dr. Byers was afraid my lungs might be hemorrhaging. The cough has gradually worsened and is not improving. The doctor has decided that the right lung will have to be operated on to take out the puss and fluid that has accumulated there. I am too sick to be moved to the nearest hospital ninety miles away in Brandon, so Dr Bigelow from Brandon General will be coming out to operate on me here at home next week. I dread the prospect but Dr. Byers says it is an absolute necessity if I am to recover. I am too weak and tired to write more. I worry so. What will happen to Bert and the girls if I die?

May 23, 1916

I am still very weak, propped up in bed writing with an unsteady hand, wanting to record these horrendous times. I have once again escaped death and am feeling a little better than I was last week. Nurse Humphreys was here for a few days, and now Beattie is able to manage looking after me and the girls. She is also doing the cooking and cleaning. Hard work, I know, and I understand why she looks forward to be going back to England soon.

The operation went well, although most of my right lung was removed. Dr. Bigelow tells me that I will have to live my life differently now. No heavy work, and I must take care to try to avoid getting colds, flu, and especially pneumonia. Above all - no more babies! Dr. Bigelow is young, clever, and a little arrogant, but Bert says he saved my life and that the operation was necessary. Still, its consequences are hard to accept.

We have had a very late spring this year. We had a lot of snow which didn't melt until April. Fortunately, the roads cleared in time for Dr. Bigelow to travel here from Brandon to operate on April 10th.

Kay continues to thrive and I long to be out of this bed so I can begin to care for her. I am not sure how I will cope when Beattie goes, but Lynda is a big help now and stays home from school sometimes to help Beattie with the house. She adores looking after Baby Kay. I fear that when Beattie leaves I will have to depend on Lynda more and more. I hate the idea of her missing school but it is very hard to find good live-in help and very expensive as well. Times are changing, and of course because of the war, women are having to do more and more work as wave after wave of young men leave for Europe. Many Melita boys have already died over there, and there are many grieving families. Our little congregation at Christ Church prays every Sunday that the war will be over soon, but it continues to rage on, gaining in intensity rather than diminishing. I am thankful that no matter what happens, I will not be losing a child to war. I have no sons to feed the war machine, thank God. I know that is a very unpatriotic thought. Bert would call it traitorous, but I will not be sharing my thoughts on war with him or many other people for that matter. Perhaps I could discuss this with Miss Oxley, but she is getting older. She does not work in people's homes anymore, although she continues her midwifery. She came to visit me yesterday and I was so glad to see her. Talking to her has given me the strength to write and to believe that perhaps I can go on after this operation.

I hate to admit to this in writing. Dr. Bigelow gave me laudanum to help with the pain and it's tempting to take a lot of it, fall into a deep sleep where the pain cannot reach me and where I can forget how weak and useless I feel. He warned me that this can become addictive and I must not become dependent on it, but it's so tempting to forget the world. Miss Oxley warns me against doing this, telling me that in the past many women have ruined their lives by becoming addicted to laudanum, including Abraham Lincoln's wife, Mary. Since talking to my dear friend, I have resolved to take less of it. I know I should throw it out altogether, but somehow, I can't quite get to that point. I am weak in mind and body. Please let me get through this dark time.

October 2, 1916

I did get through that dark time, and we are now in the midst of threshing and miraculously, I have garnered the strength to look after the children and to do my household duties. I often suffer from insomnia, but I have put the laudanum at the back of my bedside table drawer, and have promised myself I will not touch it again. I am writing this at 2 AM, not a good idea, I know, as it will be a long hard day tomorrow. I write so seldom that when I do get out my journal the thoughts and words keep flowing and the hours fly by. However, I sometimes nap in the afternoon, especially if Lynda stays home from school, which I am already planning will happen tomorrow.

The spring was very wet and the creek flooded. The rain continued through the summer and we had heavy dews and fog, more like English weather! Oh, for the hot prairie sun we are used to! The grain got so rusty that some farmers didn't even bother to cut their wheat as they wouldn't have harvested enough to make a profit. Some of our fields away from the creek did dry out enough to thresh and Bert hopes to make some money from that. Luckily, the war keeps prices fairly high. Bert keeps repeating a saying he learned from his grandfather: "The war is the farmer's friend."

Beattie boarded the train in Melita in late August to begin her long arduous journey back to England. I miss her terribly, but am happy to see her return to England. We hope to hear news soon that she will be marrying her London bobby. Bert has hired a girl named Sally Burke to help do the cooking for the threshing crew. Lynda often stays home from school to look after Baby Kay if I am feeling particularly tired. "Kaka" is so happy when that happens. She loves being with Lynda.

Because of the war, Bert had no hired man this past summer and he has been very busy with his thirty cattle, forty pigs, twelve horses, and one hundred hens. Lynda and I have the job of collecting the eggs and taking the excess milk to the creamery to be sold. We also work the separator and Lynda loves helping make the butter.

Fortunately, for a short while, Bert was able to hire a very young boy named Len Clarke who was wonderful with the horses. When I needed to take Jumper and the buggy to town, he would brush Jumper's coat so that it gleamed in the sunshine. We had short periods of wonderful weather this summer between the wet spells. He took good care of the harnesses and the buggy as well and would always have everything ready for me. If Bert had no chores for him, he sometimes drove me to town. Jumper obeyed his every wish. Miss Oxley says that some people have a magic way with horses and Len definitely has it. Unfortunately, he moved to Winnipeg with his family in September, so he was only with us for a couple of months. I miss him; even though he was only fifteen, he was a good conversationalist, interested in history, politics, and people in general. He was also very good with the girls and played with them out in the yard in the long summer evenings when it wasn't raining. Such imaginative games! I often heard Lynda and Maidie screaming with joy as they ran around the house, sometimes playing hide and seek, and sometimes "anti anti over", throwing a large ball over the low back shed roof. I was able to clean up the supper dishes and have a leisurely time sipping tea on the back step, watching them having great fun. During the many rainy evenings we played cards and simple board games around the kitchen table and I often let the girls stay up quite late. Bert would join us, especially for card game. Such happy memories!

When Len left, for a short time Bert hired another fifteen year old, Grenville Lucas, who was a hard worker but not as good with the horses and certainly not interested in the children. One evening he was bringing an empty wagon back from the field. He had to go down the hill to cross the creek at the shallow crossing. The horses bolted and headed straight toward the wide section of the creek where the water is ten feet deep. Somehow he got them turned just in time to make the right crossing, but then he hit a small maple tree, straddled the chicken fire fence, and broke four fence posts before he finally got the horses to stop. He walked up to the barn to get Bert, and later they came to the house. Grenville was shaking all over, white in the face, and unable to speak. A very frightened lad! I sat him down for tea and a piece of saskatoon pie. After eating, he was able to tell me all about his misadventure. Fortunately, he and the horses were not injured and the wagon was still in one piece. "Four good fence posts destroyed, though," Bert reminded him. I could tell that Bert was only teasing. A small amount of damage when one thinks what might have happened had the horses run into the deep part of the creek, tangled in a barbed wire fence, or tipped over the wagon. Grenville realized he was a lucky boy that evening and we were very relieved that the runaway did not end in disaster.

It's almost light. I must close this journal, and try to get a brief sleep before I have to get up to send Maidie off to school on her own. She is a very independent six year old. She trotting up the hill alone with her lunch bag in hand. Lynda will be delighted to stay home. I am sad to say she doesn't enjoy school. Sally is very efficient at feeding the threshers, and she will arrive about 8 to start her duties. We have only six men this year because of the diminished crop, so she is well able to cook meals on her own. I can look forward to a long rest this afternoon without feeling too guilty.

November 11, 1918

Armistice Day! The war in Europe is finally over! Bert, Lynda and Maidie have gone into town to join the celebration of the end of the war that will end all wars. If only I could believe that. Bert is always saying I dwell too much on the dark side of life, that I should join in the celebrations. I feel that war will always be with us, that it is the expression of the dark and violent side of human nature.

I am happier staying home with Baby Kay, actually a baby no more, but a happy two and a half year old, inquisitive and adventurous. We have a piano now, an extravagance, I know, but one of the few that Bert approves of. I play a little and Lynda and Maidie are learning some songs. Kay is already fascinated by the sounds and sits on my knee. helping me play "I'll take you home again Kathleen".

It's two years since I last found time to write, but Kay is down for her nap and the others will be in town for a long while, so I am sitting by the warm stove, having tea and looking forward to writing for a couple of hours.

This past summer we were plagued with grasshoppers. It got so bad that the council gave out poison for farmers to use. Because the war was still on, we had no hired man so Bert let me drive Jumper and the buggy into the field while he sat on the back and spread the poison. It was the first time he had ever let me help in the fields. I disliked the thousands of grasshoppers that crunched under the wheels and flew up into my face and the dust that almost choked me. However, I was happy to be able to help. I washed up with him at the outside pump afterwards, and we splashed each other with the cold well water, laughing and playing like children. Bert said "Nell my darling, we should always be like this!" I agreed but my joyful mood didn't last. I soon recover my sense of decorum, and my underlying jealousy returns. I am envious of the life Bert leads, both on the farm, and during his sometimes long forays into town. He always asks me to come to town with him, mind you, but I almost always decline, choosing to stay home with the girls. Lynda is certainly old enough and responsible enough to be left on her own with Kay and Maidie. My feelings of fear and anxiety somehow prompt me to say no. I wish I could be more carefree and happy. I seem to have a darkness inside of me.

****

It was difficult to find men to do the threshing this fall as the war was not yet over. Herb Dobbyn did it for us with a small crew. Threshing time was marred this year by two accidents, one fairly minor and the other very serious. First, Herbert Nansen caught his finger in a sprocket chain on the bagger and crushed it badly. He came up to the house and I bandaged it for him. I urged him to go to see Dr. Bigelow, who has now moved here from Brandon, but he wouldn't go, saying "Mrs. Townsend, a doctor couldn't do any better than you have." So I dressed it for him several times and he was soon back at work.

Because of the shortage of men, Len's boy Hector was helping drive the wagons, even though he is only nine. He was sitting under a heavy hay rack having lunch, when one of the men moved the rack, not realizing he was there. He screamed and screamed. I ran down to see what had happened. It was obvious that the wheels had gone over both his legs, crushing them above the knees. Bert jumped on a nearby horse and rode to town to get Doctor Bigelow. I tried to make Hector comfortable and managed to calm him somewhat. The doctor arrived quickly and after a brief examination, told us that both legs were broken. He sedated Hector and set them both right there in the field. He said though that the boy would have to be hospitalized in Brandon for a time to make sure that the bones healed properly. The hired man who moved the rack felt terrible but he had no way of knowing Hec was under there. Of course, it was a dangerous choice for a lunch spot but it was a very hot day and Hector had sought out the shadiest place he could find. He is home now and the legs are healing nicely. Dr. Bidelow said six weeks would do it and he was right. We were over to visit them last night and Hector is moving around quite well on crutches; the young are quick to heal.

It has been a hard time for Len and Eva as they have two little girls, Queenie and Betty. Twin girls died in infancy before Hector was born, so that family as had more than its share of grief. We don't visit there often, considering their farm borders ours on the west. Of course, Bert and Len get together to talk farming, and will be doing so more and more as Len is planning to purchase a threshing machine to harvest his crop as well as ours and other neighbours. He is a hard worker and has done well at farming. He and Bert have the land in their hearts and both are thriving in this place, even when conditions are harsh. Len is more of a risk taker than Bert, but in many ways they are alike.

Eva and I don't visit often, in spite of our proximity and in spite of the fact that we have children about the same age. Bert says I am anti-social and no doubt he's right. Unfortunately, Eva and I have never become close. When she first came from England I had hoped we would be soul mates, but it has not happened. This is probably my fault as I have always found Eva to be stand offish and a bit coarse. She is not a reader or a thinker. I know that sounds snobbish and no doubt it is yet another example of my inability to connect with people close to me.

I enjoy my privacy, my garden, my books, and my girls. I find enough to keep me busy without the visiting and the gossiping that some farm wives do. The reality is that I am often too tired to think of visiting. Eva is big and robust and has much more energy than I do. She goes to the dances in town with Len, and Bert sometimes goes with them. These are family dances. Lynda and Maidie have accompanied them a couple of times recently. They love to dance and Bert says they are both getting good at it. I choose to stay with Baby Kay; I am not a dancer and I don't enjoy the loud music and the smoke-filled hall. I also dislike the drinking that goes on, although it is all in fun and because entire families are there, no one drinks to excess. At least, so I hear from Bert and Lynda.

Now that the armistice has been signed, the dance halls will soon fill up with the lucky young men who will be returning from Europe. What a slaughter that was. They estimate that 100,000 Canadians were killed and buried, many in unmarked graves. That estimate is probably much lower than the reality and someday perhaps the real numbers will be made public The ones who return will definitely be ready for a good time and who can blame them. I am glad that the girls are still too young to be interested in the returnees. Of course, there are many young women in Melita anxiously awaiting the return of sweethearts, fiances and husbands. Many more are waiting for the single men to return so they won't have to dance with each other on Saturday nights. I know Bert doesn't suffer from lack of partners right now, but it might be a different story when the soldiers return. I shouldn't think flippantly of these young men; some are returning with lost limbs, damaged faces, and I am sure damaged minds after all the horrors they have seen in the trenches. The number of shell-shocked and physically wounded is not even discussed; and of course there are no estimates at all for the number of women whose lives have been altered forever by the loss of fathers, husbands, sons. I am so fortunate to have my family alive and well.

I hear Baby Kay stirring, and I must soon think of supper preparation as I know Bert and the girls will return from town tired and hungry. This diary is almost full; I will place it with the others which I secretly removed from the Underhill cellar to hide in a similar place downstairs here.

October 21, 1920

This has been a lonely summer for me as Bert has been away a lot. He has rented a quarter section of good hay land from the Hudson Bay Company about ten miles northwest of our farm, so he has been spending long days there. It is good land and the crop he hauled home in the fall was "fair", he said. Right now he is helping Len do threshing for Bill Griffith whose farm is so far away that he hasn't been coming home every night. I don't like being alone at night and always in the back of my mind I wonder what young girl Mrs. Griffith has helping her. Is she pretty? Will Bert be flirting with her as she serves supper to the crew? I know that my imagination takes over in regard to Bert and other women and probably nothing is happening at all!

In reality, the girls and I are fine on our own, and Lynda is helping the young hired man do the chores. Jack Jones is his name and I think he fancies Lynda. However, Lynda will have none of it; she has already seriously informed me that there will be no farm hands in her future. She's going to marry someone from town, although she loves our farm. Of the three girls, she is the closest to her father and he has conceded to allow her to do some of the lighter farm work. She enjoys being out in the barn with him and they are always chattering away about farming matters. Right now, Jack does the milking, and Lynda feeds the pigs, collects the eggs, and helps me with the separating. Long hours, especially if she goes to school which she does most days, although she looks for any excuse to stay home. She is waiting for the day when she finishes which will be next year. Where have the years gone? Maidie is the scholar and loves every minute of school. Even if she's sick she wants to go, whereas Lynda stays home at the slightest sign of a cold. Rainy weather, blizzards, my health, canning to do, Kay needing her. Any excuse suits Lynda. I am usually too tired to argue.

The truth is I enjoy her company and her help with the cooking, cleaning and canning.

She's also an excellent gardener and is a big help in both gardens. I have my small kitchen garden behind the house with lettuce, tomatoes, onions, carrots and some herbs. I also have some perennials there: baby's breath, yellow daisies, Shasta daisies and hollyhocks of many colours. My favourite hollyhock is such dark purple it is almost black. I'm going to save its seeds and plant more next year.

Bert's big garden is at the back as well but further from the house in its own fenced area. It is bordered at the back by the row of trees that Bert planted as a windbreak when we first bought this place. They are mature now and provide some wood for the stove. Bert plants long rows of corn and potatoes and, although I stay out of his garden completely, Lynda helps him, especially at harvest time. We have such feasts when the threshing crew is here, outside on big makeshift tables. When we are on our own, we often eat outside picnic style, sitting on blankets on the grass in the shade of the house. Sometimes we have a supper entirely of fresh corn, homemade bread just out of the oven, butter made that morning, perhaps a potato salad, and some ham. Those evenings are magical and I feel a contentment that I wish I could capture more often.

Autumn is my favourite season, even though it is the harbinger of the snows and cold of winter. Last winter was particularly cold and long, with much snow. Fun times then as well though as Bert sometimes clears a part of the creek so that Lynda and Maidie can ice skate. They love it! Bert has tried as well but he's not very good at it. He urges me to try but I am too afraid of falling. My health is still fragile, and Dr. Bigelow reminds me that I need to guard it carefully. In the summers, the girls ride Jumper and Princess, one of the workhorses that isn't too wide in the girth for them to get their legs around. The girls ride bareback. Sometimes the two of them ride Jumper; with little Kay in the middle for short, slow rides around the house. Bert of course is an excellent rider and sometimes saddles Jumper and goes for a gallop along the creek or even into town. For years he has been offering to teach me but I have never had the courage to try. I regret this terrifically as I love Jumper so much, but I am just too afraid of accidents. I think of my misadventures early in our marriage with Dolly and the buggy and I lose my nerve. Many times over the years, I have almost taken Bert up on his offer, but at the last minute, when Jumper is saddled and ready, I just can't put my foot in the stirrup. Bert gives up on me, jumps into the saddle and away he goes into town or along the creek, free in a way I am not, or will not let myself be?

However, for years now I have been very confident driving Jumper with the buggy. I love our trips to town and so I will have to be content with those. I often wish I could be more adventurous and more social, but something inside me prevents it and most of the time I am happy with my quiet life.

December 27, 1921

Christmas over for another year, and yesterday of course we celebrated Maidie's 11th birthday. The years go by so quickly. Lynda is now sixteen and is already "stepping out" with the boys, as we used to say in England. She seems to have quite a few admirers and a group of friends. Both boys and girls often come here on a Saturday night to play the piano and to listen to music on our gramophone. Bert got us this for Christmas a few years ago when Thomas Edison cabinet gramophones with the cylinder records first became available. The young people sometimes roll up the rug in the sitting room and dance. Bert has purchase quite an assortment of records. We have quite a few by Harry Lauder, whose songs are very popular with the young folk. Many records are suitable for dancing: "Shake, Rattle and Roll" by Al Bernard, a fox trot called "Feather Your Nest", a waltz called "Nights of Gladness" are all favourites. We sometimes end with a sing along. One of my personal favourites is the whimsical

"I'm forever blowing bubbles, pretty bubbles in the air
They fly so high, nearly reach the sky
Then like my dreams, they faded die."

The party ends quite early, especially in winter, as everyone has to dress up warmly for the walk up the hill and back into town. Occasionally Bert harnesses the horses to the sleigh and drives them into town which makes a special evening of it.

Just before Christmas, Aunt Cissie and Uncle Will held a dance party at their house. I decided to go as I do enjoy spending time there and feel very close to them both. It seems as though one child will be their family; their daughter Constance is a few months younger than Maidie and they are good friends. We had two sleighs; Glen Williams took one, and Eric, our hired man, and Bert drove ours. Twenty-five boys and girls were bundled into the straw with heavy robes covering them. It was 40 below but the young people were having a great time. One of the boys, Jim Tilbury, said his feet were getting cold so he was going to get out and run behind to warm up. Not a good decision, as he had on thin socks and good black leather "dancing" shoes. Luckily we were almost at Will's house, so when we all got inside into the warmth, Cissie was able to got his socks and shoes off quickly, and she rubbed his feet with snow, which prevented any serious frost bite.

Cissie had her house decorated beautifully, with a large tree in the corner of the sitting room. The dining room table with its snowy white lace tablecloth held her fancy Royal Albert china already set out for the food to be served at the end of the evening. Holly and mistletoe hung over the doorways with silver ribbons, and old fashioned Christmas cards from England were displayed on the sideboard. The sideboard also held a colourful fruit punch in a large cut glass bowl with matching glasses for refreshment during the dancing.

Of course, all the young people were dressed in their Christmas finery so it was a festive atmosphere. I had made all three girls dresses of dark green velvet, varying the style and trim to each one's individual taste. Lynda's dress is long and elegant, with a fitted bodice and a touch of white lace at the neckline. Maidie's is fancier, with a full skirt and red trim around the bottom of the skirt and around the cuffs. and neckline. Little Kay looked so sweet in hers, with a huge bow of red and green plaid taffeta at the back and a matching headband.

We danced to the music on their gramophone and Cissie played the piano. Everyone had a grand time and Cissie served a fine lunch with hot drinks to fortify us for the ride home. She had fancy chicken salad sandwiches cut into tiny triangles, homemade dill pickles and all kinds of Christmas sweets: dark and light fruit cake, date squares, and cookies decorated with red and green icing. Maidie had spent the previous afternoon at their house and she and Constance helped with the food preparation. Both of them were very proud as they served the sweets on large silver trays. The ride home seemed less cold as the wind was in our backs. We sang Christmas carols, accompanied by the large jingle bells Bert had attached to the horses' harnesses. Happy memories were definitely made that night!

But my real news and reason for writing, I am expecting another baby in the spring. Kay will be seven in February, and we really were not planning to have more, but it has happened and Bert is still hoping for his son. This baby is what Bert has been calling a "high kicker" and definitely is making its presence felt in a livelier way than the first three. "Surely a Godfrey or a Kenneth this time" he keeps saying. Miss Oxley came for a visit recently and she is not so sure that the liveliness means a boy. "I have a feeling that you will have another little girl," she confides, although I have not shared this opinion with Bert as I too feel that this will be a girl. I somehow know that I am meant to be the mother of only girls and I am more than content with that knowledge.

I feel well and although Dr. Bigelow is not happy with my pregnancy, when I visited him a few weeks ago, he said that if I am careful and get lots of rest, all should go well. "You are lucky, Mrs. Townsend. your other three are all old enough now to be a great help when the baby comes. I am sure they will all be more than happy to take care of a new brother or sister." Unlike Miss Oxley, he does not offer his opinion about the baby's sex. So we will have to be patient; the doctor says I am due in early May and I pray that I will be strong through it all.

June 7, 1922

Just a month ago, Margaret Ellen arrived. Dr. Bigelow and Nurse Douglas were both at the house for the birth. Nurse had been here for a week before the birth and will be leaving soon, as I am feeling strong. Summer holidays will soon be here so all the girls will be home to help. My labour was quite short, and by the time Bert had fetched the doctor and he got here, Margaret Ellen was almost born. She is tiny and delicate, truly a beautiful little girl. The girls and Bert of course were not allowed in the bedroom during the birth, but they saw the baby very shortly afterwards. The girls were thrilled but I saw the look of disappointment that Bert tried his best to hide when Nurse Douglas proudly announced "A healthy baby sister!"

Eric, our hired man, was also present and he was very enthusiastic about the babe. He is a recent immigrant from England and has become like one of the family. He has a cot in the back room of the shed which we call "Eric's room". I know that hired men come and go and that Eric will move on, but I have a feeling that we will always call that room "Eric's room". Eric is well educated and I know that his work here is only temporary. He talks of moving to Brandon or Winnipeg and finding office work, which would suit him better. He is a hard worker and both Bert and I enjoy his company. He is definitely the only hired man who has ever been able to discuss Shakespeare with Bert! He uses very aromatic bath salts and we can always tell when Eric is having his bath in the tub in his little room. What a beautiful smell!

As I look at Baby sleeping in her crib, I feel a very special bond with this little one. She will definitely be the last, even if it means saying no to Bert's demands. I already know she will be my favourite and a special soul mate for me as the other girls grow up and leave home. A mother is not supposed to have favourites and although I admit my feelings here, I hope that my actions will not be so open as to cause jealousy among the others. Right now I can't imagine that happening as all three girls are completely taken with Margaret Ellen. They love holding her and watching over her. We have decided that the double name is too much for such a little one, and I don't particularly like "Margaret" or "Ellen" or their own. Bert has been calling her "My little Nell", but we both agree it probably isn't a good idea for her and I to have the same name as she grows older. We are hoping that a suitable nickname will soon become apparent for her as it did years ago for Maidie. As she grows into a toddler, some character trait may suggest a good name for her.

July 13, 1922

Today was such a magical day that I want to record my thoughts even though it is late and I am feeling exhausted. When Bert got up this morning he announced: "I have exciting news. I am taking the day off and we are going on an expedition."

"We're taking the buggy and going out to the hay quarter, a long drive but it's a fabulous day for a picnic". Of course, Lynda and May had to go to school, but I quickly packed a picnic lunch. soon Baby Margaret Ellen, Kay and Bert and I were in the buggy, with Jumper excited about the prospect of a drive. It seemed he realized that this was special - not just a trip to town to get groceries and take milk and eggs to the creamery. Bert was in a happy mood, chatting and singing snatches of his favourite songs. He hinted that this might be our last buggy trip to the hay quarter. I didn't know what he meant. Are we are not going to rent the hay quarter any longer? Or will there soon be some other means of transportation? Two or three motor cars have recently appeared in Melita, Model T Fords. They seem to be noisy, stubborn things, difficult to start and belching out fumes. They are quite lovely to look at though, with their polished chrome and leather upholstery. Could we be getting one of those, I wondered. Bert refused to say.

The day was glorious, not too warm, and because we've had such a wet spring, there was lots of water in the sloughs. "Not much hay this year," Bert said but he didn't seem too concerned. Orange tiger lilies were everywhere we looked, on the green slopes leading down to to the water-filled ditches beside the road, and in the distant hay fields. Meadow larks and robins sang. The prairie is so beautiful in mid summer, especially when spring rains have greened the land. We stopped for a picnic on a rise of land that wasn't damp, and spread out the blankets. After lunch, the babes both fell asleep and Bert and I did too, eventually, after making love right there on the prairie, something we have not done since Lynda was conceived all those years ago. I am still nursing. I hope there is no chance of pregnancy but this afternoon I didn't care. If only we could have more times like this afternoon!

October 20, 1922

Today Bert's hint of a surprise on the day of the picnic became very evident. He drove into the yard late this afternoon with a new Model T Ford! It's a beautiful vehicle but I still feel very nervous riding in it. Bert admits that he doesn't feel quite safe driving it yet. He jokes that he still feels inclined to yell out: Get up and whoa, Jumper!"

Of course, we still have the horses for farming. Bert says he has no interest in the farm machinery - the tractors and other implements that are just appearing in the advertisements in the farming magazines. "I will never give up my horses!"

November 16, 1924

"Bunny" is now two years old and she is certainly living up to the nickname that Bert gave her when she first began to walk. "Quick like a bunny rabbit" he said and the name immediately "stuck". She may want to trade it for something more sophisticated when she is older, but for now she is definitely "Bunny". She is small and agile and gets around the house so quickly that I really have to watch that she doesn't get into mischief or into dangerous situations. I have had to be strict with her, especially around the hot stove. She did have one minor accident when she reached out for balance and touched the oven door. Luckily the burn on her hand was a surface one and it taught her to avoid the stove. This past summer we really had to watch her when we were outside and were very careful to keep the house yard gate latched at all times. Otherwise, she might have been out and away to the barn or even worse to the creek before we could catch her. Of course, Kay, Maidie and Lynda were home in the summer to watch her for me or I would never have been able to tend to my garden properly, or to get the canning done this fall.

A big change for us: Bert has finally found suitable man to help him full time. He has been searching for years for the right man. Of course, all our hired men have been seasonal workers and they move on to other jobs eventually. A few have been unsuited to the work and Bert has had to let them go after a few weeks. All our hired men have lived with us, so that room and board was part of their wage. This arrangement worked alright in most cases and I grew used to having an extra man at meals. They slept in the tiny room at the back of the area where we have the milk separator so they were not really in the house. Some, like Eric Russell and the young Jack Jones became like members of the family and I was sad to see them leave. However, the fact that they were so transitory meant that there were sometimes quite long periods of time when Bert had to do all the chores and the farm work himself. Therefore he was very happy to find a man named Harry Boscow. The girls laugh at his name and think its very suitable for someone who spends a lot of his time with cows! Harry is married with two children and lives in a little house on the road at the top of our hill. He is able to walk to work and Bert has decided he is a capable "all round man"; he is good at milking and handling the horses, so Bert has decided to hire him year round. He is originally from England, and is small and quick moving. He is polite with me. and likes to joke with the girls. We hope that he will be able to work here for many years to come.

November 26, 1924

Curling: what a ridiculous word! I wish I had never heard it, that the game had never been invented! Last winter, Bert was never home. He has gone mad for curling. Because we now have a full time hired man, Bert has more leisure time and has chosen to spend most of it curling. He says it's a great game and he's good at it. In fact, he's already been promoted to skip, whatever that means. He and Bill Cobb are now busy promoting a farmers bonspiel, which I gather is a weekend event where a lot of teams play against each other until a winner is somehow determined by Sunday evening.

I went into town one day to see what curling was all about. Grown men with brooms hurling heavy granite rocks from one end of a sheet of ice to the other. They shout a lot and apparently the aim of all this is to get one's rock closest to the centre of a circular design which is painted on each end of the ice. There is also sweeping with brooms that seem very similar to the one I use to clean the floors at home. Also a lot of shouting and camaraderie, including nips out of bottles of whiskey stashed on the sidelines. The rink as they call it is partially enclosed, but I was still freezing standing on the sidelines. Of course, the curlers move around a lot so it's not as cold for them and I'm sure the whiskey warms them as well. Oh yes, to confuse the issue even further, the teams as well as the building are called rinks. I was so cold and confused, that I left before the game was over, taking Jumper and the sleigh and leaving Bert to get home on his own.

He did eventually get home, a few minutes after midnight. When he came in I was sitting by the stove reading. I find it difficult to go to sleep until he comes home, a habit I wish I could break. When he is out late at night, my thoughts sway between anger that he's enjoying himself without me to worry that he may have had some sort of accident and be lying in a snow drift somewhere. As he came in, he said rather gruffly: 'Where were you? I expected you to stay until the end of the game so we could go home together!"

"I was just too cold," I explained. I decided not to add that I was also bored and somewhat disgusted by all the noise and the nips of whiskey. "How did you get home?"

"Harry drove me to the top of the hill and I walked the rest of the way in the pitch dark." He pushed past me into his bedroom and slammed the door. Since Bunny's birth, she and I have been sharing the spare bedroom. I told Bert that I needed to be near her and that our room was too small for her crib. Of course, we both know the main reason is that I no longer want to share his bed. The doctor has said in no uncertain terms that another pregnancy would kill me, and I grew afraid after Bert and I made love on that magical picnic last spring. I have decided that complete abstinence from sex will be the plan from now on. Obviously, Bert is not happy with this plan, but the truth of the matter is that I have grown to dislike sex. It is too much associated for me with guilt and the threat of death. I am ashamed to be thinking like this and am even more reluctant to write about it. I know there are means of birth control; Dr. Byers has mentioned them to me briefly. I am not really interested.

I wish Bert and I could still be close without the sex, but I know that for him it is not possible. I have worried all our married life that he sometimes has other women, and now of course he will have even more reason to be looking for someone else. Bert is still very handsome, one of those men who has stayed slim and youthful looking into middle age. I on the other hand have become too slim, skinny is the word. I am frail looking; often I look in the mirror and realize that I look severe and unhappy and years older than my age.

I am fairly sure Bert will never leave me and the girls but I also know those blue eyes of his are always in search of a woman who may be interested. I am pretty sure that some women have been interested in the past, but I will not let myself become obsessed with jealousy.

On to happier things:
The girls are growing up and I enjoy seeing their friends. Sometimes a group of Lynda's friends come for an evening. We clear out the furniture in the sitting room to make room for dancing and some parlour games. As I think I mentioned in an earlier entry, Bert has been collecting a varied selection of records for the gramophone and some of them are fun to dance to. I sometimes play the piano as well and the girls and boys dance or gather around to sing. Maidie and Kay are allowed to stay up and they love to join in. We always end with a ridiculous

but hilarious game called "grunt" which sounds so silly I am almost embarrassed to write about it. It is silly, but I love playing it. It is one of the few times when I seem to forget my cares and just have fun. We all get in a big circle and one person is blind folded and put in the middle of the circle. That person is twirled around to disorient him or her and then the circle begins to move quietly around. At some point the person in the middle point his finger at someone and says "GRUNT!" That person must make a pig-like sound and the person in the middle has to guess who it is. If he guesses correctly, that person goes in the middle. It's much more fun in reality than it is on paper! We always end the evening with salmon and ham sandwiches and a cake or cookies, with iced tea or on special occasions, a birthday or Christmas, some of Bert's homemade chokecherry wine. Bert often takes the guests home in the sleigh or if the weather isn't too cold, the young people enjoy walking back to town, thus prolonging their evening of fun.

Lynda has a very lively group of friends, and of course they are at the age where couples are beginning to form. Lynda seems very keen on George Cochlan, a rather shy boy with a jolly round face and twinkling eyes. He is well mannered, polite and a good conversationalist. He works in the hardware store and has told me he would someday like a manage store of his own. I worry about Lynda getting too serious about him as she is very young, only nineteen. Of course, I can't help but think back to the days when Bert and I were courting. Our feelings for each other were so overwhelming that we couldn't, or didn't, control them. When I see George and Lynda dancing together and looking lovingly into each other's eyes, I don't know whether to be happy or sad. But I know I must let her live her life. She will be making choices and leaving us now that she is finished school.

September 21. 1925

It's happened - the inevitable, I know. I have been expecting it and yet when it happened and how it happened were a surprise and a shock to me. Lynda and I have always been close - even when she was a young teenager at an age at which some mothers and daughters go through difficult times, Lynda always talked openly to me about what was going on with her friends and her life in general. She had become quieter lately and I knew that she was upset with her father and me because we have been trying to discourage her from an early marriage to George. George decided a few months ago to move to Grand Rapids, Michigan to work in a friend's store. Lynda wanted desperately to marry him and go with him. She is so young and I know it was partially selfishness on my part that made me oppose the idea so strongly. I didn't want her to move that far away: another country, another world. She knows that I left my family at her age to follow Bert to Canada. I understand why my attitude made no sense to her. At any rate, Bert and I told her that we wanted her to wait until next summer and that we would not consent to the marriage now. When George was settled, he could come back for her and if they still wanted to marry, they could plan a church wedding next summer. After many tear-filled conversations, she and

George agreed to wait. George got busy making plans to leave on his own, packing, saying his good byes to friends and family and buying his train ticket on the Soo railway line that stops in Melita on its way down to the States.

Last Saturday Lynda, Bert and I went to the train station with George's parents to see him off. The train sits in the station for about half an hour before continuing south, so we had time for good byes. There were tears and hugs and at last George climbed the steps up to his carriage. At the last minute, Lynda said to me: "I'm just going to jump on so we can have a bit more time together." Before I could answer, she was gone. The train was due to leave in 15 minutes and soon I began to feel very nervous. Where was she? Bert asked the conductor for permission to go look for her and so he too boarded the train. He had to get off, though, when the train was about to leave.

"Where is Lynda?" I shouted as he came down the platform toward us.

"I couldn't find either of them anywhere.. The bathrooms are locked because people are not allowed to use them when the train is in the station so I don't think that they could have hidden there, but there was no sign of them anywhere else."

I could not believe that Lynda would be so deceitful as to plan this, but as Bert helped me in the buggy I realized that I had to accept it. I fought back tears and we drove home in silence.

It was a sleepless night for me. What was Lynda thinking of? I worried until dawn streaked the sky outside the bedroom window. Then I climbed wearily out of bed and made a cup of tea. I felt unable to face the day. Of course Bert got up at his usual time, had a quick breakfast and went out to do the milking and other chores without a word to me. I finally found the energy to call the girls and to make their breakfast of boiled eggs and toast and make their lunches. "Where is Lynda?" they all asked at once as they came into the kitchen. I broke into tears and told them what had happened.

"That's called eloping," Maidie said. "I think it's very romantic."

Bunny, too little to have an opinion, just laughed at the obvious excitement in her sisters' voices. Soon Kay and Maidie were trudging up the hill to school, lunch pails in hand, chatting as though nothing had happened.

Bunny and I sat at the breakfast table for a long time, Bunny happily drawing in her book with some new crayons. Suddenly, there was a knock at the door. It was Sam Cleveland from the telegraph office. He handed me the telegram in his hand. "Good morning, Mrs. Townsend!. Good news, I hope". I knew that the telegram message would be known all over town almost as quickly as I had read it! I sat down at the table and took a deep breath.

Got off train in Fargo. STOP. Married by a justice of the peace. STOP Going to Grand Rapids today. STOP. Lynda and George.

Of course had they planned this all along! I have to accept that Lynda is gone and hope for her happiness. I feel an empty place in my heart though and know I will be lonely and sad. Michigan is not that far away and I hope that Lynda and George will be able to come home next summer for a visit.

Bert will be a little angry about Lynda and George's deception, but of course he will accept the inevitable and continue his busy life as if nothing has happened. He refuses to discuss any of it, saying it's now in the past and that I must get over being upset. If only it were that easy. Bert's stoicism seems hard hearted to me although I know that as usual he is being realistic.

I will try to concentrate on day to day things and devote myself to my other daughters. The way time flies by, Maidie will be leaving home as well. I must get used to seeing them leave. Kay and Bunny are still very young and they need me. I must not be sad for their sakes.

November 1, 1926

Wet weather — so much rain! Luckily most of it has occurred since the crop was cut. Bert hired Jim Seaver to help with the threshing,. He is fresh off the boat from Scotland, and quite a character. Because of the wet weather, the men had a lot of time off, and Seaver had some interesting pastimes. He played a lot of cards with Bunny, who at four was just learning simple games and was delighted with his jovial chatter. He also loved to shoot ducks. We had some good dinners as a result. If there were no ducks, he'd shoot pigeons. I didn't approve, but Bert said it was all in good fun. One day when they were threshing, Jim found five young skunks in a hay stook. He caught them, and skinned them in the pig pen, feeding the fat skinless skunks to the pigs. He smelled of skunk for weeks, but the council gave him two dollars for each skin, so he thought it had been worth it.

In spite of Jim's attics, he was a good worker and the threshing went well considering how wet the season had been. We had a lot of wild oats in some of the fields, and it was so damp ii was black. plenty of feed for the stock, Bert said. Fortunately, Bert had planted a lot of barley and the market for it was very good at 46 cents a bushel. We harvested and sold 2000 bushels.

I'm going to try to write today of a secret in my life, one that I have avoided discussing in this journal, as shame has prevented me from finding the words. Or is it fear of discovery? That someday someone may find this journal which I keep hidden? That Bert or one of the girls will read these words with horror? I also will try to write about an incident in my life which is not a secret, which is fact, many people know about, an incident that no doubt was gossiped about by all our friends and neighbours for many weeks after it occurred.

The secret began when I nearly died ten years ago, when I began taking laudanum and felt the wonderful escape it provided, from pain, from reality. I said then that Miss Oxley had warned me about its addictive qualities and urged me not to take any more than was absolutely necessary to help the pain I felt after the operation. I wrote then that I vowed never to depend on its power again, and that I hid the remaining powder in the far corner of the drawer in my bedside table. I also mentioned then that I should have thrown it away but some weakness prevented me from doing so.

When life became difficult, when Bert left, for a few hours or a few days, when I was too tired to go on and retreated to my bed in the afternoons, I used it, not often at first, but it is addictive, just as Miss Oxley warned and gradually I found myself using it more and more. Dr. Byers does not seem to have the same reservations about its use, and because I use only small amounts, I don't have to ask him for it too often. Of course, I have done this secretly, paying for it out of my household money. Luckily, it is not expensive and Bert does not suspect anything. Or at least, I hope he doesn't. He has questioned me sometimes about my lack of energy or lack of focus, and then I swear never to take it again. I am weak, though, and a short time later when the girls are at school and Bert is in the fields, I sneak to my bedroom for a "nap".

I think Lynda suspected something, but she never questioned me about it. Now that she is gone, I am lonelier than ever and fear I will become even more dependent. I have no one to talk to about this; Miss Oxley is the only one I have ever really shared my feelings with, and I am too ashamed to discuss it with her. Sometimes I wish I were a Catholic. Perhaps the confessional could be a place to admit to this shameful habit and perhaps get some guidance. I cannot imagine talking to Reverend Barth about anything personal. We attend church regularly as a family, and I find our Anglican service calming and comforting. Reverend Barth's sermons are thoughtful and intelligent; he is gentle and well educated, but he is very reserved when he comes for tea, which he does quite regularly. We chat about weather, crops, and parish events, and about his family. I tell him about the girls' progress in school and serve him whatever I have baked that morning: banana cake, butter tarts, matrimonial squares, or chocolate brownies with walnuts. Not exactly a suitable setting for discussing my addiction to laudanum.

And so it continues. I know that it contributed to a recent episode in my life when I lost control of my emotions and my actions. For some reason, my birthday on June 19 always seems to be a difficult and sad day for me. I worry that I am aging much faster than Bert and that my health will deteriorate to the point where I will not be able to look after the girls and perform all my household tasks. When Bert suggested going out to the Legion dance to celebrate, I refused to go and expected him to stay home as well. We had a serious argument and he stormed off to town by himself. I felt upset and lonely, even though the girls were upstairs, Bunny and Kay sleeping and Maidie with her nose in a book.

I am so ashamed of my actions that night that I cannot write in detail about them. I know that actions like these are unacceptable, and that I should stop taking laudanum. However, thinking that and writing about it are not the same as actually doing so. In fact, I have used even more in the months since my birthday, trying to shut out the terrible memories of that night. After Bert left, I went outside, nd placed some Bert's most precious possessions in a big pile on top of the woodpile farthest from the house. After some difficulty I got the fire started.. The conflagration grew quickly. Soon flames shot high into the twilit, purple blue of the summer solstice sky.. I fainted. When I opened my eyes, Bert and Maidie were leaning over me. I could see the neighbours around me, whispering to each other.. With utter shame, I realized that the flames and smoke would have been visible from town. Local men were busy dousing the fire with pails of water from the outside pump. I saw the horror and fear in Maidie's eyes, and I could read the disgust and anger in Bert's face as he and Maidie carried me to the house and put me to bed.

I can write no more, and in fact may rip out these pages. This journal is almost full. I am going right now to hide it with my first journal, down in the cellar, tucked far away in a corner behind some old canning jars.

Journal Five

Depression, 1926-1939

November 10, 1929

I have not written for years, and in fact did rip out my last entry although I have kept those pages, hidden away in my cellar. My secret continues, but I am able to function and my health is "holding" although I do not have as much energy as I would like.

Last winter was very cold with continuous blizzards. Some days were beautiful; brilliant sunshine made diamonds on the hard snow drifts in the fields, although it was bitterly cold, often 40 below. Then another blizzard blew in, and we were trapped inside for a day or two. The school closed, so the girls could stay home, quite happy to read and play cards in the warm kitchen. Bert went out only to do essential chores: feed the animals and milk the cows. The hens stopped laying so he had no eggs to collect. He had strung a rope which extended from the house to the barn so he didn't lose his way when the snow on the ground and the falling snow blended around him in a world where only white existed. He said it was quite an adventure, but I was always glad when I heard him come up the steps to the house.

When the weather cleared enough, Bert spent most of his time at the curling rink. He went to the Souris bonspiel and said he had a lot of fun, although they didn't win quite enough games "to get in the prizes". In fact, I have seen no prizes yet from all this curling! Bert enjoys it so I know I shouldn't be negative about it. It helps to pass the time when the winters are long and cold.

The spring was late, but we had hot weather in May, so it was dry for seeding. The rains came just at the right time in June and July, so we had a bumper crop. Lots of celebrating when the threshing was done.

But then in late October — disaster! The radio was full of very dire news, but "Black Tuesday", October 29th, was the worst. The New York stock market collapsed completely. I am not really sure what that means although Bert explained it simply by saying that everyone is selling and no one is buying. People are going bankrupt and the effects are being felt all over the world. Business men in the States have been committing suicide by jumping out of their high rise office building windows. It seems that when they learn that their riches are reduced to nothing, they feel that death is their only option. It seems to me that fortunes aren't everything, that surely these men must have wives and children and somehow could start a new life? But then what do I know about life and how to live it properly? The possibility of suicide has occasionally entered my mind as well, but thoughts of my girls and of Bert bring me back to my senses.

As farmers, we have plenty to eat but no money. The price of eggs has rapidly plummeted down to five cents a dozen, because most of the farmers have eggs but few people have money to buy them. Bert is gradually selling off the cattle at very low prices because it doesn't make sense to spend money feeding them when there is no market. Pork has down to five cents a pound, so we have been eating a lot of pork rather than selling the pigs at a loss. Wheat is now twenty cents a bushel, oats, two cents, barley nine. Bert keeps saying that selling grain at these prices hardly pays the shipping bill.

Bert said to me last night: " We are really up against it, Nell. Although I hate to do it, I will have to let Harry go. We just can't afford to keep him full time. Luckily, I'll be able to hire able young men just out of school to work part time. They are eager for whatever wages we can afford to pay, as there are no other jobs available."

So a succession of wonderful young men have helped Bert at different times: Pop Quane, Jim Coates, and Wilf Menzies. They were happy to work for 25 cents a day with meals included, and I am more than happy to cook for them. They are always enthusiastic about my meals and compliments fly around the dining table. "Wonderful shepherd's pie, Mrs. Townsend!" "I just love the saskatoon tarts!" "I'd work here just for a piece of your lemon meringue pie!"

****

Maidie finished Grade 11 at sixteen after taking the last four grades in only two years. The teachers decided that otherwise school would have been just too boring for her. She got some of the highest marks in the province in her final exams and then went to business college in Brandon where she excelled at all her courses. She was awarded a certificate for being the fastest typist in the province when she graduated from business college. In spite of the poor economic times she got a job right away when she returned home. She is working at Mr. Crerar's law office and making good money. She loves her job and although she lives at home, she is always out with friends. Bert keeps hinting that she should be paying some attention to some of the nice young hired men, but she laughs at the suggestion. I have seen her and Wilf having some earnest conversations as they share a cigarette on the verandah after supper, so perhaps there is a spark there. Speaking of sparks, I am a bit disgusted that all the girls, except Bunny of course who is much too young, have started smoking. It's all the rage among the young people and Maidie says it shows sophistication. Bert has never smoked so I am not used to it but they are independent young women now and have to make these decisions for themselves. Hopefully there's no harm in it!

Kay is in Grade 10 and wants to go to normal school in Brandon when she finishes high school. I think she will be a good teacher; her talents in art, music, and drama will be put to good use in the classroom. Beginning teachers have been making about forty dollars a month; even after paying room and board, that's a good wage. Teachers are always needed, especially in the one and two room rural schools. If the bad economic times continue, of course, wages may be non existent and Kay may be working for room and board!

Hopefully, the world will right itself after the terrible events of this fall, and our children will not have to struggle with economic hardship. I feel rather isolated from it all, but Bert says that the world is getting smaller and smaller and that what happens elsewhere effects everyone, even on farms in the middle of the Canadian prairie.

September 8, 1930 - Grand Rapids, Michigan.

I can scarcely believe we are really here: my first trip away from home since we went to England all those years ago. Bert decided in August that we should take a road trip to the States to visit Lynda and George. They usually come to visit us in the summer, but George hadn't been able to take time off work because his boss had been sick. So, out of the blue, Bert said one evening: "Let's surprise Lynda by driving down for a visit". All the girls including Maidie were able to come. Maidie has already told me that she is able to take a few weeks off from her law office, and Kay and Bunny will be fine missing a week or two of school.

I was a little bit skeptical about the plan, but Bert was able to hire Harry to look after the place for a month We packed the Model T and away we went. Fortunately, it's a sedan with lots of room for the five of us and our luggage. It turned out to be a grand trip - 1250 miles! Bert has is keeping detailed records of our mileage and of course our gas expenses. It took five days to get here! The weather was scorching hot, but we had such fun: windows open, songs and games, picnics by the side of the road, nights spent in little roadside motels, inexpensive but clean with friendly owners who would tell us where to get a reasonable evening meal. Not like my home cooking, everyone kept saying, but we survived the change in diet. Kay and Maid did not bring shorts so they both cut off their trousers. A bit daring, I thought, but they actually looked quite stylish. Luckily, I brought some summer dresses for Bunny and also for myself as I have yet to allow myself to wear trousers. The girls keep telling me I have to stop being so old fashioned, but so far I have resisted.

We telegrammed Lynda two days before we arrived. She was so excited! She and George were able to rent part of a friend's house for us to stay in, as their place is tiny. She cooked a grand feast for us the day we arrived, although I will say that the Swiss steak she had prepared had turned to mush by the time we actually sat down to eat supper. We were all so busy telling Lynda and George about our trip as we sat around in their back yard that we forgot completely about eating, until Lynda jumped up and ran into the kitchen where she rescued the dinner from the warming oven. We enjoyed the meal immensely anyway. We were so excited about being all together that we hardly noticed the food. Lynda had made an angel food cake for dessert and she served it with delicious whipped cream and strawberries. Oh yes, she had also iced it with coffee flavoured icing, topped by toasted almonds, which is my recipe which we often have for birthday celebrations Lynda's birthday was last Tuesday, so we found some candles for a grand celebration.

We plan to visit here for three or four days and then drive home via Chicago. George is able to get a few days off and he and Lynda plan to drive their car as far as

Milwaukee, so Kay and Maid will probably go with them that far. Bert says we have to be home soon for the harvest, so we will not be lingering along the way.

This holiday has been so good for me. We have had such hilarious times all together in the Model T and I realize that we should do more of that kind of thing when we are at home. Somehow, though, at home, so much gets in the way. I worry about meals to be cooked, cleaning to be done, weeds growing high in the garden. However, I do recognize that it is mostly things inside of me that stand in the way of my having plain ordinary fun: my natural reserve, my frail health, my intense jealousy and resentment towards Bert.

I must go now. Lynda is planning a picnic excursion to Aman Park in the Grand River Valley. She tells us this is a very large park with many picnic sites and walking trails. Apparently in the spring the wildflowers there are amazing, At this time of year, the trees are beginning to display the fall colours that Michigan is famous for. There is also a good possibility we will see some wildlife: deer, wild turkeys, squirrels, perhaps even a pair of foxes who have their den there. I am sure the day will be wonderful!!

November 12, 1934

I can scarcely believe that more than four years have gone by since I last took the time to write here. Of course time is not the real reason; the truth is that I have not had the inclination to write. I was so happy during our trip to Michigan, but our life since then has been hard. The depressed economy continues to be a great problem everywhere, but for prairie farmers, it is the continuing drought which makes our lives almost unbearable at times. The dust gets into everything, the clouds build up on the horizon, promising rain but bringing only thunder and more wind. I often retreat to my bedroom, close the doors and windows, and reach into my bedside drawer for the escape that awaits me there.

Bert of course soldiers on. When we got back from Michigan that fall, the crop was not heavy but prices were still holding their own; wheat was still over a dollar a bushel, although the price of other crops was unsettled, and farmers were getting very nervous about what the future might bring.

To make matters worse, when we got home from our trip, the house was crawling with huge ants. Not quite as bad, perhaps, as the infestation of mice we faced when we first moved here, although they seemed to bother me more. They were all over the kitchen and into all the food. I hated them! Bert kept saying that the winter would fix them, but I told him I was not waiting for that. So he went to work and found their nest in under the verandah. We gradually drowned them out with lots of soap suds. Such a relief! I was able to take possession of my kitchen in time to feed the small threshing crew we had that fall.

In 1931 we had three dry months in the spring. Although we had a good rain in early July, it was not in time to save the grain crops. Bert said we were fortunate that the wild millet and sweet clover grew in spite of the drought and he was able to mow feed for the cattle. There was no threshing that year and prices continued to go down. The years to follow were even worse. Bert had let Harry go and he did chores alone during the winter. He kept only a few cattle but even for those few, feed was scarce.

Bert and Maidie both spent the winters curling. Maidie has become very good at it, and now has her own team or rather she is skipping her own rink to use the correct terminology. I go to town to watch them sometimes, and envy them their love of the game. It is a very social sport and they have a lot of fun. It certainly keeps Bert's mind off the hard times. Maidie is in a young and carefree time and has been able to hold on to her job at the law office. She's very fortunate to have Mr. Crerar as an employer, one of the few in Melita who can still afford to pay someone to help him. I guess bankruptcies need lawyers!

I envy them their distraction with the game. I wish I had learned, but like horseback riding, it's something I have never had the courage to try. Speaking of horses, Jumper died last week. He was twenty eight. I feel as though I am mourning for a child, although probably I shouldn't use that analogy. He was an important part of my life for so so long. I miss him terribly. This summer, Maidie had a last adventure on Jumper. One day after work, she decided to go for a ride. Pop was taking a break from plowing, so she asked him to saddle Jumper so she could ride up to visit her friend Elsie who lived down by the river on the other side of town. He gladly did so, happy to spend a few minutes in Maidie's company. They are close in age and I am always speculating about boyfriends for Maidie. So far, though, she seems uninterested.

Pop helped Maidie up, but just as she left the yard, one of the barn cats ran in front of Jumper. The sudden movement must have frightened him and he reared. Maidie slipped sideways, catching her foot in the stirrup. Luckily Pop got to them in time and was able to grab Jumper's harness and help Maidie down. Maidie got right back into the saddle and continued on with her planned ride to town. Bert told me about all this later, saying that it could have been a nasty accident if Jumper had got running and dragged Maidie with her.

Kay also had a recent accident riding Jumper. She did a lot of riding last summer with her friend Evelyn, who has a lively roan horse named Barnaby Rudge. One beautiful July day they decided to ride over to visit cousin Queenie. It's about a mile and a half to Uncle Len's farm, just a nice distance for a short ride. I was out in the garden when I saw Evelyn riding down the hill, leading Jumper. I ran out to meet her, feeling sick inside. "Where is Kay?" I screamed. Bert was in the barn and came out running when he heard me. Evelyn explained in a shaky voice, "We were galloping along the section road when somehow Kay fell off. She is lying beside the road, crying and saying her arm hurts." Bert said, "Evelyn, thank God you had the good sense to ride back to our place so quickly. I will go get her in the car." He ran over to the Model T and roared up the hill. I took Evelyn into the house and sat her down for a cup of tea. She was badly frightened but we had both calmed ourselves before Bert came back with Kay. We went out to meet them. Kay was huddled in the back seat, her face streaked with tears and her arm twisted in a very awkward position. "I'm taking her to Dr. Byers right away; I think she's broken her wrist." Bert told us without getting out of the car.

When they returned a few hours later, Kay's arm was in a cast. She had broken her right arm just above the wrist. It was a bad break and Kay was so shaken by the accident that she has not ridden since. Bert is still trying to convince her that she should try riding Princess, one of the farm horses that is small and gentle, but I think Kay's riding days are over. Maidie still loves riding and takes Princess out often. Of course her small misadventure on Jumper was not very serious, but Maidie is stronger than Kay, in mind and body both. Kay is delicate and very sensitive. More like me, perhaps?

People are beginning to refer to these years as the dirty thirties and dirty they are. Dust is everywhere in the house; I have given up cleaning except for the kitchen. I spend my days trying to keep dirt and insects out of the food we eat. The wind blows constantly and the summers have been extremely hot. If I open the door for even a second, the dust blows in and last summer the air was filled with millions of grasshoppers. They destroyed entire crops and died by the thousands in the creek. They even got into our drinking water! My garden was eaten overnight, and I struggled to keep those horrible insects out of the house.

The drought continues, and last winter there was not much snow, so no moisture on the fields even in the spring. Last spring the government supplied seed to those who needed it. Bert sowed 300 acres with wheat but the grasshoppers began to eat it as soon as it came up. He and the hired man spread the poison that was being given out by the council but they were fighting a losing battle. Even as they were spreading the poison, they could see millions of hoppers coming across from Kirkup's farm, heading for the only good thirty acres of green wheat that we had. Bert thought they were beat, but Jim Coates, who was working with him at the time, had an idea: "Let's mow it right now!" And that's what they did. By the end of the next day, they had cut and gathered three good loads of feed from that thirty acres. From then on, they cut feed from all over the farm, in the small patches that somehow escaped the grasshoppers. In the first week in July, Bert said: "That's it! The hoppers can have the rest!" He had been coming in from the fields with grasshoppers stuck to him everywhere, in his boots, under his collar, in the cuffs of his pants, even in his hair where they had somehow crawled up under the straw hat he wore.

There was no threshing this fall and my garden was nothing but weeds and thistles. We are fortunate, though, in that we still have chickens, eggs, milk, butter, and can still feed our cattle and our pigs.

The pigs took a notion to go wandering at night. Our neighbour up the hill, Marsh Jones, knocked at the door one night about midnight, startling us both. Bert went to the door, and Marsh, quite angry, said, "Bert, I think all your pigs are feasting in what's left of our garden". So they went down to the barn to check, and sure enough, not a pig in sight! Bert went up the hill with Marsh to chase them back home and to secure the pen so they couldn't escape. Apparently, Bert had told Jim to keep the three mother pigs with their thirty little ones inside the barn during the day so that the little ones would not get sunburn. He let them into the outside pen at nights, and they escaped through a break in the rails, always coming home to be sound asleep when Bert went out to feed them in the mornings. Bert is always saying that pigs are the cleverest of animals!

In the fall, Bert and Len took Len's truck and drove up to Newdale, north of Brandon, to collect vegetables. That area had had rain and the people there had more than enough produce, so they got a whole truckload which the town council distributed to those who needed food. There were many other carloads of vegetables, fruit, clothing and bedding sent free to people who needed them. Everything was stored at the municipal hall and distributed accordingly. The generosity of those not affected by the drought or the grasshoppers has been overwhelming.

I find it heart warming to know that many people care about our situation. However, somehow that alone does not alleviate my own personal depression and I still find myself escaping to the solitude of my bedroom where I close the curtains, lock the door and find my solace in laudanum.

September 5, 1935

Our first grandchild! In the spring, I took the train down to Michigan to help Lynda before and after Paul was born on April 2. Paul Townsend Cochlan is handsome and healthy and we are so proud of him! I spent the spring and summer months with them, and those months were some of the happiest times of my life! Just holding Paul and helping care for him has restored me so much in mind and body that I feel I can face life again! Lynda was very weak after the birth, and she experienced an alarming loss of vision. Her doctor assured her that this happens to a small percentage of women after childbirth, and that sight is usually restored to normal after a few weeks. When we left, however, Lynda was still having a lot of difficulty with her vision and none of the doctors she has seen have ben able to give her a proper diagnosis. We can only hope that her vision will improve gradually.

I was able to spend a lot of time with darling Paul and I know he will always be a special person in my life. George is a very caring father but he needs to spend long hours at his job. I spend a lot of time worrying that Lynda's sight loss will make it difficult for her to cope now that we are so far away. Lynda was feeling great when I left though and assured me that her side vision is perfectly clear, so that she is able to manage well.

The spring here was dry and dusty, but Bert is managing fine. In the spring, he was asked to sow some corn for feed. The council gave him seed and he planted ten acres. Apparently, the corn grew ten feet high and he cut a lot of feed to be used by farmers who need it. I would have loved to see that corn. Bert was very proud of it and tells me it was a sight to behold.

In fact, Bert decided to take on more land. Bert has been so frugal over the years that financially we are still alright, even though many around us are losing their farms to the banks. He has rented one such farm, the old Demarais place, 1000 acres bounded on one side by the Souris River. All but 200 acres has gone back to grass. Bert cut hay there and got a good first crop, but then heavy rains came in the first two weeks of July, and of the of the 200 acres he had seeded, he lost 50 acres due to flooding. The rest of the summer was hot and sultry; a lot of the wheat rusted and was not worth threshing. No money made yet!

November 12, 1936

Last month, Maidie married Lew Davidson, a surprise for both Bert and me. Bert was very much against the idea and tried his best to persuade Maidie to change her mind. I still don't know whether to be happy or sad about it all. Lew is unsuitable in many ways: he is exactly twice Maidie's age, 52 to her 26, and has been married twice before. His first wife died under mysterious circumstances. They had three small children when Eleonor died, and rumours circulated saying she died during an abortion that went terribly wrong. At any rate, Lew found a housekeeper to look after the little ones and he eventually married her. It seems it was just a marriage of convenience on Lew's part, as for many years it was well known that Lew had another woman, a Mildred Livesley who worked in the bank. There was speculation that once the children grew up, Lew would get rid of his housekeeper/wife and marry Mildred. To everyone's surprise, he ditched Mildred, divorced his wife, and eloped with Maidie. They were married in Fargo, North Dakota, and are now back in Melita, living in the same house that Lew has lived in for years. His children, of course, are all grown: they are in their twenties now, the same age as Maidie. In fact, they were all her school chums. No doubt Lew and Maidie are the talk of the town right now. Divorce is almost unheard of here, and the fact that Lew was so open about his relationship with Mildred Livesley shocked the townspeople for years. Many tongues will be wagging now that Lew has married "one of the Townsend girls."

Although it sounds rather arrogant to say so, I know that all four of our daughters are highly thought of in the town: great achievers in school, hard workers, and of course they are all quite beautiful. I don't kid myself; I also know that Kay and Maidie are probably known for their partying as well. They love to dance, they smoke and drink and have good times. All of this is great fodder for the gossips, and small prairie towns are great places for gossips to meet and embellish on stories like this one.

On the plus side, though, Lew has a good job as manager of the Beaver Lumber store and he is a handsome man, very athletic and fit. He went to university briefly on a football scholarship, and excels at baseball, curling, and other sports. He also likes to play cards and is good at it, so Bert and he sometimes have a game of nap or crib together. However, Bert hates Lew's politics. Lew is an active supporter of the Liberal party and of course Bert is a died in the wool Conservative. I leave the room if politics becomes the subject of conversation.

Maidie is very obviously in love with the man. She literally glows when they are together. In spite of everything, I am cautiously and secretly happy that they are married, although I would never tell Bert that. I hope and pray that they will have a good life together, although realistically I know that the age difference probably means that Maidie will be a widow when she's still young. I'm not sure Lew will want to have another family, which is sad. Maidie does not discuss this with me, but I think she would like to be a mother someday.

Anyway, their relationship and marriage have taken our minds off the weather and the bad economic times. Agin the spring this year was hot and dry. The mosquitoes and black flies were a real problem. Swarms of them circled the horses as they were working in the fields, getting in their ears and noses. This made them very hard to handle, and although Bert is an expert with horses, he often came in from seeding, tired and frustrated, feeling sorry for his precious horses. Again this fall the crop was very light although we have lots of hay for feed. However, prices for grain, pigs and cattle are slowly improving and Bert says we are getting back on our feet.

We seem to be over the worst years of drought and grasshoppers. It is still bad though in parts of Saskatchewan, and there are people moving here from that province, bringing their horses and cattle with them.

Sometimes they take over the farms that were abandoned in 1933 and 1934. Nearly half the farmers left this area and many did not return.

Bert tells me it is hard to figure out what crops to grow to make the best money. He decided to plant fall rye last year. He thought it was a safe crop to depend on although the jack rabbits liked to eat it in the winter. Bert has a great sense of what works in farming and sure enough, he harvested 5000 bushels and got 75 cents a bushel for it. He said "we made a little out of it" to use his words. I don't see the accounts and don't have access to the bank account so I really don't know the profit margin. Bert fed some steers for the June market and he said they fetched a good price, as did the pigs he fattened. We are beginning to feel that the desperate times are perhaps in the past.

One sadness though. The weather was so hot and muggy this summer that something infected the horses. We kept watching them, but they slowly sickened and became so weak they couldn't stand. The sickness struck our dear horses regardless of their age and we eventually lost five of them. We had any sleepless nights, both of us near tears. Our horses have been so much a part of our lives; it is heart breaking to see their suffering

We knew that the same thing was happening on neighbouring farms. It was a serious epidemic. Bert does not believe in spending money on unnecessary calls to medical people, be they doctors or vets. In fact, he is generally distrustful of their ideas. He feels that his years of practical experience with animals, especially with horses, allows him to deal with problems effectively. Usually, I agree with him, but this disease seemed very serious. Luckily, a new young vet had moved to Melita in the spring and Bert had met him a few times in town. "He seems like a practical fellow", Bert said, and finally agreed to call him.

Dr. Morris arrived quickly and after examining the horses, he told us that they were suffering from sleeping sickness. The technical name for it is equine encephalomyelitis. He also told us an interesting story about how the virus and its cure were discovered fairly recently. Apparently in 1930, a number of horses in the San Joaquin Valley of California died of a mysterious encephalitis. Karl Friedrich Meyer, a well known biologist, investigated but was not able to isolate the pathogen from necropsies of horses that had been dead for some time; he needed samples from an animal in the earlier stages of disease. When his scientific team heard of a horse that appeared to have encephalitis, they went to the farm to investigate. The horse's owner, fearing the loss of his horse, threatened to shoot the scientists if they didn't get off the property immediately. However, Meyer talked quietly to the farmer's wife and was able to convince her that the horse was dying anyway, and he offered to pay her $20 if she would secretly signal him when the farmer was asleep so that they could examine the horse. She agreed as $20 was a great deal of money at the beginning of what was to become known as the Great Depression. Meyer and his colleagues hid in the bushes until she gave the signal.

They crept into the barn, euthanized the horse and stole its head. Back in the lab, they successfully isolated the virus from from the brain tissue. And from there, they were able to find an inoculation to stop the virus.

The vet explained that the sickness was so widespread that the Council was supplying the drug to inoculate all the horses in the district. Therefore the vet was able to inoculate our remaining horses right away. Once we did that, the epidemic stopped and thank goodness, we lost no more.

Journal Six

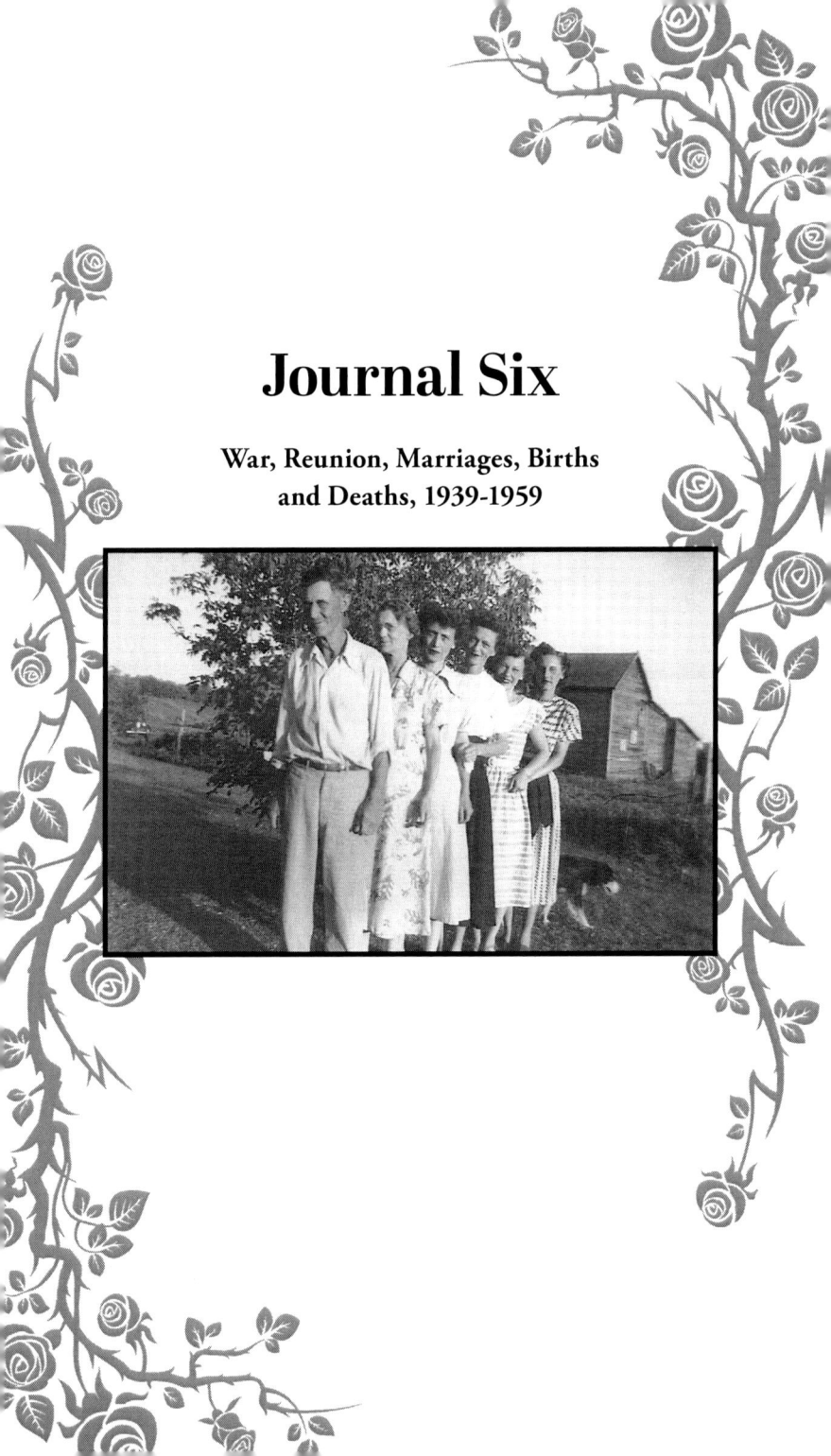

War, Reunion, Marriages, Births
and Deaths, 1939-1959

November 20, 1939

War again in Europe. To me, it seems as though the first great war, the war to end all wars ended quite recently and they are at it again. Hitler, the German leader, has invaded Poland and the news reports say this is just the beginning. However, Bert tells me it has been good for us economically. Our rye crop was harvested early this year and 3000 bushels of it were already in the elevator waiting to be sold in the open market. Bert was offered 23 cents a bushel. He told me he had a premonition to wait awhile and see what Hitler was up to. The next week Hitler marched into Poland and the price of grain skyrocketed to 80 cents a bushel. Bert is planning to sell it in small parcels throughout the winter and will probably make four or five times what he was offered before war broke out. I find all this very distressing but Bert says farming is a gamble and who doesn't like to gamble once in awhile.

December 15, 1940

More than a year has rushed by since my last entry. Why do I so often choose the dreariness of winter to write here? Perhaps because I am so often alone. Bert of course is at the curling rink, his home away from home once the snow flies. Or perhaps because writing offers something else for me to do, an alternative to going up to my bedroom, crawling under my quilt and opening the drawer on my bedside table to lose myself in laudanum. Just writing that word down is tempting me. I will resist the temptation to stay here by the warm stove with my cup of tea. I will think back over the past month and find pleasant memories to write about. Of course there have been many pleasant days, especially in the summer when Lynda and Paul visit from Michigan. The last two summers they have come up on the train which means they can stay for a couple of months before George drives up to fetch them in August.

Paul takes our minds off the problems of the world. He is four and his summer visits to the farm are weeks that I live for. He is such a handsome boy, with his sandy hair and those bright blue eyes —Bert's eyes –- the same eyes I fell in love with years ago. He is a bit chubby now, but I think he will be tall, taller than his parents. I am not sure why I think that: I just know it in my bones. He talks a lot and he and I have many conversations. He is very inquisitive about everything around him. The farm is so different from his home in the city that when he first arrives he literally runs through the house and the yard asking questions as I try to keep up with him.

Paul is also very interested in everything about the barn, the horses, and the pigs. He has many questions for Bert which Bert delights in answering. No doubt he sees in Paul the son he never had. They go off to the barn hand in hand and I know that in the back of his mind he sees Paul, little as he is, as a possible heir to the farm. Although we don't discuss this, I know that neither of us can bear the thought of this farm being sold to someone outside the family.

Bert and Paul spend many hours together, yet another reason for me to be jealous! I know I should not begrudge their time together. Paul loves helping to feed the pigs and chickens. He rides with Bert on the plough or the hay rick, perched up on the hay. He is delighted with the the stone boat as Bert bumps along over the field. Of course at four Paul isn't actually doing any work but he loves being out with his "Dodo" as he has taken to calling Bert.

Bert confided to me one night after Lynda and Paul had gone to bed that he'd had a bit of a misadventure with Paul and one of the horses, the tall sturdy one we call "Old Bob". Apparently when Lynda and I were in town doing the grocery shopping, he decided to see how Paul would like to ride old Bob.

"I put him up on Bob's back and Paul was delighted. Suddenly, Bob started to shake himself fiercely. Perhaps he thought Paul was a fly, he was so tiny and light. Anyway, I lost my grip on Paul's arm and he slid right off Bob's rump. Bob is a big horse! It was a long way to the ground for a little guy! But Paul cried only for a few seconds, more frightened than hurt. I picked him up and whispered that this would be our secret from Mom. So, Nell, don't tell Lynda. She might never let me take Paul to the barn again!"

Paul is such a lively one, always into a bit of mischief. One morning this past summer, he locked me in the outdoor biffy and ran away. I didn't think he could even reach the outside latch but he did. I heard him laughing as he ran back to the house. I had to yell and yell before Lynda came out to rescue me. She was very angry with Paul and he got quite a serious spanking. I felt badly about the incident then; I cried and told Lynda she was being cruel. Reflecting on it now, I realize that Paul needs discipline at times, and locking his grandmother in the biffy was probably one of those times.

Paul brightens my life and I miss him so much when he leaves and the winter stretches ahead. I know that I am very fortunate that he and Lynda can visit for so long every summer. I love that time of year: the berry picking, the gardening, the picnic suppers in the side yard with the daisies and the baby's breath blooming beside us. We often eat a cold supper, usually ham or chicken with potato salad, corn on the cob in August, perhaps butter tarts for dessert. I love the long evenings when it stays light until 10 or 11 and Paul is allowed to stay outside with us, watching the sky for that first star. Paul loves it when we whisper together:

> "Twinkle, twinkle little star, first star I see tonight
> I wish I may, I wish I might
> Get the wish I wish tonight!"

Our house is full and lively in the summer. Bunny is still living at home and working at Eyers Furniture store where I know she is a valued employee. She is grand company; she and I are very close and in many ways she has become the soul mate I predicted she would be when she was a baby.

Kay is now in Ottawa with the civil service. She left her teaching job when the war started. And she has plans to join the Wrens, now the official name for the Women's Royal Naval Service. I believe that some women did see active duty with the Wrens in WWI and I know that Kay hopes to go overseas which worries me somewhat. She has always been a dreamer and I am not surprised that she wants to expand her horizons beyond one room school houses in remote areas close to home.

Maidie and Lew seem happy enough. Lew has a good job as manager of the Melita Lumber Store, so Maidie doesn't need to work but she does some part time work in the law office. No grandchildren there. Lew already has three grown children and three grand children. So at fifty five he is probably content with his life as it is and doesn't want to start another family. They recently got two lively springer spaniel puppies whom they've named Punch and Judy. Training them has been a lot of work, but Maidie assures me that it's a lot of fun as well. Maidie often walks down for a visit with the puppies on a leash. They are getting to be a handful as they are very lively and are growing like weeds. They love to swim and go in the creek at every opportunity, much to Paul's delight. He toddles in to the water after them and laughs delightedly when the pups shake and soak him with water.

Sitting by the creek watching Paul and the puppies, my daughters by my side –- happiness indeed! The world seems full of joy in the summer sunshine, but when the darkness of winter descends, sadness engulfs me. The days are so long. It's only three o'clock. Bert probably won't be home until supper time, maybe late. Perhaps I have time for a nap after all.

March 30, 1945

Where have the war years gone? For me they have past in a dark haze, although I have not had to bear the sadness of losing sons, the way many mothers have. So many young men dead, many more wounded seriously. The war has left a gaping hole in the community here, and I am sure it's much the same everywhere. The Battle of Britain, Pearl Harbour, Dunkirk, the endless voices coming from the radio with more and more bad news. The years crept by somehow and even the summer sun did not save me from despair.

At the end of July 1942 we had a very serious hailstorm; huge hailstones came pelting down for ten minutes, destroying every head of grain on 450 acres. Windows were smashed in the house and the shingles on the roof were ruined. We had no insurance on the crop or the house. The entire experience was very eerie. After the hail it got really cold and the air smelled like winter. Then as the temperature rose, the fog rolled in. Lynda and Paul were here, and luckily we were all safe inside. After the storm, though, Paul soon got over his fright and was delighted to play in the piles of hail beside the house, which took a few hours to melt.

Bert said it was the knockout blow. We hadn't had a really good crop since 1928. Luckily we had bumper crops in '43 and '44. In '44 Bert told me proudly we had a $5000 crop so we are definitely making money after many long years. Cattle prices were also good: $300 for a1000 pound steer. The war, as Bert predicted, turned into an economic boom for farmers.

The happiest moment for me through it all has been the birth of my first grand daughter. We were all surprised when Maidie told us she was pregnant. I had assumed that they had decided not to have any children. She is 35 and after ten years of marriage, I think she was very surprised herself. Lew is 60 now and has three grown children and five grand children!

As if to magically coincide with the war ending, Maidie had a baby girl on March 1. As if to mirror Winston Churchill's inspirational V for victory sign, the baby was born with a bright red birthmark on the first two fingers of her right hand, her very own V for Victory sign. Surely a positive sign that this little one will be victorious over the hardships she encounters in her life.

Maidie had a good pregnancy and an easy delivery at Mrs. Forsythe's nursing home. There is no hospital in Melita, of course, but Maidie and baby had good care and were home after a few days. She and Lew are both delighted. They have decided to call the baby Lynda-Lew, after her aunt and of course her daddy. Quite a long name for a little one, which I am predicting will soon be replaced by some nickname.

I have been spending long hours at Maidie's house, helping with the cooking, cleaning and carrying for Baby when Maidie is resting. I am thrilled to have another girl baby to love, and she reminds me so much of Maidie when she was first born. Of course when Maidie was born I was too ill to enjoy her properly so I am making up for it now. Having this new life to help care for has banished my feeling of despair and I do hope that I will be able to continue without the retreats to my bedroom and the healing power of laudanum. It is very addictive though and I know the journey will not be easy. I feel uncomfortable writing about this, and I must go. I hear babe beginning to stir in her crib.

December 15, 1947

I am delighted to write that the last two years have been full of joyful events. I have been too busy to do much of the retreating into the hazy world of escape I spoke of when I last wrote here.

The events all happened in such proximity to each other that I hardly know where to start.

Two years ago, Bunny moved to Gladstone, a small town quite far north and west of here. She got a good job in a furniture store there and soon brought home a handsome man for us to meet. He is a farmer from a big German family and he and Bunny are obviously very much in love. So on the evening of October 27, 1946, she became Mrs. Oscar Otto in a candlelight ceremony in our little Anglican Church. At last I got to see a daughter of mine have the wedding I had always dreamed of. Both Lynda and Maidie ran off to the States to marry, so I have had to wait a long time for the romantic wedding I'd always dreamt of. Bunny looked absolutely beautiful in her long white gown, a bouquet of red roses, very petite next to Oscar, who is big and broad and strong.

We sometimes call Bunny "Madge" the name she uses as a married woman in Gladstone. Oscar and she stayed with us for a year and Oscar helped Bert with the farm. I know that he hoped that this might eventually lead to his taking over the farm some day. Oscar is a very strong willed man and I think had some recovering to do from his war experiences. He was in the invasion of Europe and got a Victory Cross for bravery at Dieppe. Although he appears strong and brash, I sometimes see sadness in his eyes. He and Bert did nor get along, and so he and Bunny have gone back to Gladstone, where Oscar is working with his brothers on their family farm.

Although having Bert and Oscar in the same house was sometimes awkward and uncomfortable, I was able to escape up to Maidie's house because a few short weeks after Madge's's wedding, Maidie had twins! "What a commotion!" Bert kept saying. And indeed it was a very busy time. Little Lynda-Lew was only 18 months old and although she was "as good as gold" most of the time, she wasn't much more than a baby when the twins arrived. She naturally showed her jealous feelings towards the new arrivals sometimes. They consumed so much of their mother's time. Indeed all our lives became centred around them.

They were two months premature, and when Maid went into labour so early there was a lot of confusion at the nursing home. The doctor knew there were twins, but he'd neglected to tell Mrs. Forsythe who was assisting at the birth. After the first one, she thought the whole thing was over so there was a lot of running around as they prepared for the second one. Of course if this had happened in the hospital, they would have both been placed in incubators as they were only three and four pounds. They are very frail and their skin is so delicate that they can't wear clothes! The doctor said it was dangerous to move them all the way to Brandon to the hospital and so they are at home over the heat register. We rub them with baby oil and handle them only when necessary to feed them. No diapers to change but lots of sheets to wash.

The days go by in a flurry of activity centred around these two dear babies. The doctor told us when they were born that it was uncertain whether they would survive. They are both little fighters. Now they are over a year old, and all danger is past. They are beginning to talk, and show signs of walking soon. They are not identical twins but Maidie dresses them alike. I have been busy making clothes for them and they are busy growing out of them. They are still a lot of work but it's the kind of work that I am more than happy to do. The twins are constant reminders to me of how precious life is and how we must hold on to what is important.

We had another wedding in the family in October. Kay finally arrived home after her time in Halifax during the war, although she spent several months with Lynda and George in Michigan before she came back here. She was very sad and subdued when she first arrived and I heard her crying in her bedroom at night. She won't talk of it but Lynda did tell me when she was home in the summer that Kay had had her heart broken by some man in Halifax. I think the details of that relationship will stay forever a mystery to the rest of us; I wish Kay would talk about it with me but we are not close when it comes to discussing personal matters. I will not push her for information.

Soon after Kay returned to Melita, she started going out with Scotty Fraser, whose parents we have known for years. He too was in the war and although he is handsome and debonair, I sometimes see an underlying sadness in him. He was in the airforce and I know he took part in many bombing missions over Germany. No one discusses the details of this, of course, but there are whispers of many civilian casualties in places like Dresden. I can't help but think what it must have been like for those young men up high in the clouds dropping bombs on cities full of women and children. He stayed in the airforce for some months after the war, flying planes across Canada on some sort of after the war victory celebration which seemed very bizarre to me. Scotty is soft spoken and very likeable although I am afraid he drinks too much. Alcohol is an understandable escape for young men as they try to blot the terrors of the war from their minds.

Anyway, he and Kay had a whirl wind romance. They started going out in August and got married in October. Kay did not want a big wedding and refused to get married in a traditional white gown. After some argument, she consented to a church wedding with a small reception here afterward. She looked lovely in an aqua silk suit and did concede to wearing a short veil. I loved her going away suit, a forest green wool with leopard trim, which really complemented her delicate beauty. It also showed her flare for the unusual. She's quiet, our Kay, but her impulsiveness sometimes leads to unrealistic decisions. I wonder about her choice of husband. He's wonderful and fun but is he the one for Kay? Enough of this! I have worried about all my girls when they married, but they all seem happy and content with their lives.

I found having fifty people here for the wedding meal very tiring, but fortunately Bunny was here to help. Maidie was too far advanced in her pregnancy to be on her feet much, so Bunny and I did most of the cooking. We had a cold buffet and everyone seemed to enjoy themselves. Kay and Scotty left right after supper to go to Vancouver for their honeymoon. Apparently, Scotty has some connections in BC and may be getting a job in a hardware store. Another of my girls gone so far away; I doubt that I will ever be able to travel to British Columbia. Everyone says it's beautiful but I have seen pictures in magazines of the mountains there. "Forbidding" is the word I would use for that landscape. Nothing like the soft Dorset fields of my childhood. Nothing like the Manitoba prairie I have grown to love in spite of the hail, the blizzards, the grasshoppers. When I think of the sunsets, the tiger lilies, our nine horses in the pasture beside the house, I feel content to have chosen this place as my home.

Writing about the horses and the land has made me think of recent conversations with Bert about the future of farming. Most farmers now have tractors and huge machines called combines. Grain farming is being done on a large scale because in order to justify the high cost of machinery, farmers have to have more and more acreage. Bert will not give up his horses. I know some people say that he is too cheap to spend the money on machinery, but I know how much he loves the land, his horses and the old ways. He says he hopes to continue mixed farming on a small scale and will probably get out of grain altogether. It is already hard to find teams to harvest the old fashioned way, although Milton Taylor still has his threshing machine and will continue as long as he can.

We will also plan to keep up our large garden. We love to have the fresh produce and I still do a lot of canning and preserving. As the girls continue to leave home, and our house is not as full of young people, we need less and less. And of course, no more huge threshing crews to feed. Those days are part of the history of the prairies now and will remain in memory only. Sometimes I think that this journal would make an interesting record of an era but then I realize it is much too personal to share with anyone, let alone strangers.

Bert and I spend quite a lot of time reminiscing about the past, about the girls growing up, funny little stories that stick in our minds. We laughed so hard last night over tea; somehow we both got thinking about Maidie and her friend Billy and the potato beetles. Wilhemina was her real name but she was always Billie and still is even though she now lives in faraway Toronto and has a career in some sort of financial company. Anyway, to get back to the potato beetles. One year, when Maidie and Billie were six or seven, Bert had planted acres of potatoes in the big garden. He hoped to get a good price for them, perhaps as much as $1.50 a bag. Milton Taylor had a digger back then, and with a team of four horses, the stone boat, and a few helpers, the huge crop could be harvested quickly. However, that spring, when the potato plants were still small, potato beetles began to appear in huge numbers. They are pretty bugs, large brownish orange beetles with dark spots. Their size and colour make them easy to see, but there were so many of them. Bert knew from experience that if he didn't pick those bugs before they laid their eggs on the leaves, there would be thousands of little ones. He could then spray poison on the entire field, but he didn't like to do that. So to save the crop he was determined to pick the beetles before they laid their eggs. A tedious job and very time consuming. Billie and Maidie were playing in the garden as they often did, so he decided to recruit them to help. He made a game of it and also offered a little money. "I'll give you a penny for each and every beetle you pick!" Bert really didn't think they would take it seriously but with a can and a piece of shingle, they worked and worked. They picked 160 bugs each! In Bert's words, they made a clean sweep of it and saved the crop. We both remembered the happy proud looks on those little faces when Bert paid them for those potato beetles!

August 25, 1949

I am totally exhausted. Our entire family has been here this summer for a proper reunion.

For a week earlier this month, all four of our daughters and their families were here together, the first time that had happened since they left home to marry and have families of their own. Kay and Bunny have no children of their own yet, although Bunny whispered to me in the kitchen one day that she is expecting a baby and is very excited. She doesn't want to share the news with the rest yet, and of course I will respect her wishes. I haven't even told Bert.

Maidie of course was here with all three little ones. Lynda-Lew at four was enjoying being the centre of attention much of the time, trying to upstage the twins, who are so adorable at two. Jane and Nora are each developing distinct personalities. Of course even as newborns they looked different; Nora has always been blonder and a bit thinner. Jane has dark auburn hair and a more "rounded" look somehow, although she's certainly not chubby. She is less shy than Nora, and is learning to talk more rapidly. Nora blushes so easily: her face breaks out in red blotches at the least bit of attention! Unfortunately, Lew was not around much during the week of the reunion, so he is not in any of the pictures we took. Bert and he continue to look at life differently; Lew seems to find it hard to spend time here. Or perhaps he just decided to let Maidie have time on her own with her sisters! And how they have visited! I tire easily, so I often went to bed early. From but from my bedroom upstairs, I could here them night after night, laughing and getting louder and louder as the evening progressed. Of course I know the hilarity was occasionally helped along by large glasses of rye and water. Lynda's voice is especially strident, and I can her her often. Bunny is the next loudest; Maidie I can hear only sometimes, and Kay's quiet voice is not audible. It was wonderful to hear them visiting so happily; our house now is all too silent most of the time. Bert and I don't talk to each other much anymore, seeming to find it easier to lose ourselves in silence.

During the four days the girls were here, we had many picnics in the yard, swims in the creek, walks to Fairy Ring and East Cliff. We were joined one day by the extended family: Will and Cissie, with their daughter and family. There were thirteen adults and five children, quite a large group to feed. Of course, the girls all helped and we had a simple cold buffet meal with lots of salads: potato, some jellied fruit ones, tomato aspic, all the the recipes that my daughters are beginning to refer to as "the old prairie standards". Will my grand daughters even know about such things when they grow up? Will they remember matrimonial cakes, butter tarts, brownies with marshmallow icing? Will they be interested in my old recipes fifty years from now?

Bunny has just sent me a large packet of photographs from the reunion. They are wonderful! That is, everyone looks wonderful except me; I look staid and old. I tried to avoid the camera, and did so for most of the informal pictures. However, Bunny insisted that we line up for some formal pictures, and I couldn't avoid being in those. The girls all looked so lovely in their summer finery. They are all so slim and really in the prime of their lives. Each of them has developed a way of dressing that to me suits her personality; Lynda and Bunny tend to more conservative clothing, in beiges and browns. Having said that, I notice that in the formal photographs Bunny has a wonderful striped dress in navy and white, with a sash around her waist, still showing no sign of the baby to come. Maidie and Kay are the "fashion plates" in the family although their styles are very different. For the family photo, Maidie wore a flowing black skirt, a white blouse with a high collar to show off her cameo pendant. Kay looked sweet as usual in a pale pink and white dress with a large lacy collar. Will future generations of our family find these photographs in a box in an attic somewhere? Will they be treasured or forgotten? What is it about this reunion that has triggered these kinds of questions about the future?

December 27, 1952

So many years since my last writing. I can't believe I have let the years slip by without recording so many important events. We have threshed our last crop the old fashioned way which makes Bert very sad. He refuses to have machinery on the place, not even a tractor! Financially, we could probably afford to make the change, buy more land, and more machinery. Truthfully, Bert tells me very little about our finances so I don't really know much about the money situation. However, I do know that he will not give up on his beloved horses until he is too old to farm. He will continue with "mixed farming" which is really the term for those of us who for various reasons will not make the change to larger farms. Bert plans to plant a few acres of oats for feed and get a few more cattle, pigs and hens.

We have two more grandchildren, both born in 1950: Michael to Bunny and Ian to Kay. We see Michael every few months; they are here for Christmas right now and will stay for a couple of weeks. Michael is a beautiful looking child, a bit chubby, with curly hair and a flashing smile. He is a handful though, always on the go and already a little defiant towards authority. He loves to play with Maidie's three girls but I know they find him too rambunctious for their type of playing. The girls of course are older, and are quite quiet in their activities. They love to read books, draw pictures of horses, and play school together. I think they will grow up to be librarians or teachers! Michael, on the other hand, is wild. He is still a toddler, three on January 12. Hopefully, he will change as he grows older. We saw Ian this past summer when Kay and Scotty made the long drive from Kamloops, BC. He is a serious little guy, quite a contrast to Michael with straight hair, wiry frame, and solemn grey eyes. I hope Ia and Michael get to spend time together as they grow up. They live thousands of miles apart though so we will have to plan lots of family reunions so that our BC grandchild will know his family. Because I moved so far away from my family in England, our girls never had a chance to know many of their cousins. When Kay and Scotty were here this summer we had such fun: picnics in the yard, horseback rides, sing songs and walks along the creek. East Cliff, which is really just a slope into a ravine, seems giant to the grandchildren now, although I am sure as Ian grows up in the middle of the mountains, he will see the prairie with different eyes. It's hard for me to imagine their journey here through the Rockies; the trip took five days and sounded very adventurous to me.

I noticed a tension between Kay and Scotty this summer. Scotty disappeared sometimes and when he returned, it was obvious that he had been drinking. I heard whispered arguments coming from the spare bedroom and Kay would come out later with reddened eyes. She of course did not discuss any of this with me. I regret that my reserve when the girls were growing up always prevented me from discussing really serious issues with them. I think they didn't want to worry me because I was so often ill, and I never pressed them into serious discussions.

I try to concentrate on the positive. On the happy times we are all able to be together. I am so fortunate to have Maidie and her three darling daughters close by. In the summer, the four of them come walking down the hill almost every day. We have picnics and the girls swim in the creek. They are really just paddling in the shallows by the stepping stones. They are not allowed to go in what they call "the deep end", which is the wider part of the creek past the weeds where the beavers have created a deep pond. Bert swims there sometimes to cool off after a day in the field. He also breaks the beaver dam every few weeks to keep the water flowing but during the night, the beavers work their magic and the sticks are in place once again.

We spend many happy hours down by the creek. We always take the salt shaker for the leeches. Lynda-Lew is seven and is quite grown up about the leeches. She refuses to scream and run to me when one attaches itself to her toes; instead she walks calmly to where I keep the salt shaker in a bag beside me, gets it out and shakes salt on the leech's tail, laughing in delight when it scrunches itself into a little ball and falls into the sand. The twins are only five and are naturally a bit squeamish about the leeches, especially when they stretch themselves out to their full length of about six inches and wiggle through the water close to where they are paddling. However, in the heat of a prairie summer, water is water and once the leeches disappear under stones or wherever they live when not attached to human flesh, the girls go back to splashing happily in the water. If the day is not too hot we sometimes cross the creek and take a picnic up to the shady spot under the Big Elm, or perhaps continue farther along the shady narrow path as far as Fairy Ring. There we spread the blanket and enjoy the cool quietness of the shade as we snack on ham sandwiches or crackers and cheese. During those magical times, I often think about the first time I walked here, when we bought this farm forty years ago. Lynda and Maidie were almost exactly the same age as my granddaughters are now. The years melt away as I stare up into the branches of the elm and into the blue of the prairie sky.

December 20, 1953

I am finally able to get out of bed for a few hours each day. Since August the months have passed in a haze. I collapsed in September with a ruptured hernia and had to be rushed to the emergency ward at Brandon Hospital. But that is not the story I want to record right now, although I will write about it in more detail later.

Bunny and Michael had come home for a few days in August. Oscar was too busy on the farm to come with them, but they wanted to visit with Lynda and George before they went back to Grand Rapids. Paul and his girlfriend Pat were also here, helping Bert with the haying. On the evening of August 23, Maidie and the girls were here as well – a reunion for three of the four sisters. We were all sitting around the kitchen table after dinner, enjoying tea and cookies, when the phone rang. Bunny answered and almost collapsed on the floor at the news she was hearing from Oscar's brother. Apparently, Oscar had been out in the fields when he collapsed and was rushed to the hospital. The doctors feared polio. Cases of this dreadful disease had been reported in the last few years We know now that this was to be a major epidemic which killed many and crippled even more. There were thousands of reported cases in 1953 alone and about 500 deaths.

Oscar was being transferred to the hospital in Winnipeg. Bunny threw a few clothes together and George drove her to Gladstone that night. This was the beginning of a terrible time for Bunny. It was soon evident that Oscar was paralyzed from the waist down and would probably not walk again. Bunny stayed in Winnipeg for months until Oscar was able to come home.

On September 15, I collapsed in the kitchen, feeling an acute pain in my stomach. Bert got me into bed and phoned Maidie. She and Doctor Kaye arrived a few minutes later. Dr Kaye examined me and said immediately that I had a ruptured hernia which needed to be operated on right away. I didn't want to be rushed by ambulance to Brandon Hospital; I was afraid I might die on the way. Surely I could stay here and Dr. Kaye could look after me. I knew he was not a surgeon, but I felt in too much pain to consider facing the long trip to Brandon and being subjected to the "knife" of a strange doctor. Then Dr. Kaye said "Nell, I will arrange for Doctor Bigelow to oversee the operation. I knew that he was semi-retired now but I remembered him as competent and kind. I felt somewhat better about the possibility of going. After three long days, Bert, Maidie and Dr. Kaye made the decision that the move was absolutely necessary for my survival. The ambulance arrived and Bert went with me to Brandon General, where he was able to get me into a private ward. Unfortunately, we soon learned that Dr. Bigelow was out duck hunting and wouldn't be back for a few hours. Even through my pain, I remembered that the last time we called Dr. Bigelow he was out at a Christmas party. Perhaps he was such a good surgeon because he knew how important it was to take time off to have some fun! Dr. Cromarty, the surgeon on duty, said I was an emergency case and he wanted to operate immediately. I wanted to wait for Dr. Bigelow's advice and Bert agreed.

Bert left to have a meal and in a few hours, he returned with Dr. Bigelow. Bert and he were chatting like old friends. Bert was saying, "It's thirty five years since you last operated on my darling."

"I remember it well," Dr Bigelow replied. "Dr. Byers and I in the sleigh in that snowstorm, me driving the horses and him looking over the side to keep his eyes on the edge of the road so we wouldn't tip over into the ditch. We got there just in time!"

Dr. Bigelow examined me quickly. I was in terrible pain but I remember hearing his booming voice: "Get her down to the operating room; it definitely is an emergency." Dr. Cromarty did the operation with Dr. Bigelow overseeing it, although of course I heard all this from Bert much later. Apparently the operation lasted about two hours, with Bert waiting patiently for the "verdict" as he called it. Dr. Cromarty finally emerged from the operating room and declared: "It was a success, Bert, and with proper care, she should recover completely." He even showed Bert the portion of my intestine that they had removed.

The doctors both suggested that I needed constant medical care, so Bert arranged for three special nurses to be with me in shifts. All the medical staff were determined that I would survive this. So began my long convalescence. Bert had to go home for the threshing. Luckily Paul was able to stay to help him, although he was expecting a call from the US army soon and would have to go home. America, unlike Canada, still has compulsory military service. Lynda came up from Grand Rapids by train and stayed with me in the hospital for the many weeks it took me to recover. In fact, she is still with me as I write this months later. Bunny was able to come to visit for one night, leaving her vigil with Oscar in Winnipeg General. I was so happy to see her, although she was very tired and sad. Oscar would be in hospital for months and there was still no movement in his legs. Luckily, Michael can stay with Maidie, which makes things much easier for Bunny. Of course, Bunny was worried about me as well. The doctors said I was improving but not out of danger yet. I tried to assure her that I was on the mend and in very good care. The nurses were so good to me and I formed a bond with Nurse Brown, who was young and lively. She was a reader and so she and I discussed books we both enjoyed and she sometimes read to me. She reminded me of my dear friend Miss Oxley who had been so good to me when Maidie was born.

Finally the doctors said I was well enough to have more visitors so one Sunday Bert brought Maidie, the girls, and Michael in for a wonderful visit. The girls had been asking constantly when they could visit and it was so lovely to see them. Bert has just bought a new car, a navy blue Prefect, so they were able to come "in style". I didn't hear this until later, but apparently they got lost on the way home! Imagine, Bert getting lost on these familiar prairie roads! He is embarrassed when the story is told but the girls thought it was such a great adventure that they told me as soon as they could. It was dark, they said, and somehow Bert took the wrong turn at Virden. They were almost out of gas by the time they realized they were on the wrong road and turned back. A journey that usually takes an hour and a half turned into a three hour odyssey over unnamed back roads!

A long six weeks crawled by and finally the doctors said I could go home. Bert came in to Brandon on the bus and rented a large comfortable car to take me home as the Prefect is very small. Needless to say, we travelled by daylight and had no further adventures, although of course during that trip I didn't know about Bert's misadventures a few weeks earlier. He didn't mention anything about it!

It was lovely to be home even though I was still very weak. Fortunately, Lynda was able to stay all winter to look after us. I was still bed ridden so Lynda did all the cooking and cleaning as well. She was happy to be able to help. George was fine on his own and very supportive of her staying with us. Bert was busy with fall ploughing and doing lots of curling. He and Lynda often played cards at night and sometimes I felt well enough to sit by the stove and have tea and a bed time snack with them.

George arrives tomorrow to be with us for Christmas. Maidie, Lew, the girls and Michael will be joining us for Christmas dinner and I feel well enough to enjoy the festivities and the food. Having the children here will be wonderful, although I feel very badly that I am not strong enough to help with the preparations. Both Lynda and Maidie are good cooks and they have been busy baking for Christmas, using mostly my recipes, so I know the food will be delicious and we will have a very happy time together.

As I write about this time of my life, I wonder why I have once again been so close to death and have survived. Of course, I am very thankful to be alive, to have more time to spend with my family, hopefully to see my grandchildren grow older.

I try to concentrate on the future, but my mind keeps slipping back to the past. I am constantly caught by flashes of memory about Bert: the happy times when we were so in love, the difficult times when jealousy overtook me. My memories range back and forth. I see the magical picnic in Devon when we first met; I see Bert's blue eyes, I hear the brook bubbling by us, I taste the sweetness of the dessert my mother had prepared all those year ago. I think of the elation I felt as we danced around the fairy ring with our two darling daughters the day we bought our farm. Then the dark times creep in, though, and they erase the happy memories. I see the flames the night I burned all of Bert's favourite things. I imagine the fire truck screaming down our road, the neighbours chattering around us even though I know that by then I had fainted and know of those events because Bert told me of them later. Even though I am ashamed, I think too often of the many times I have lost myself in the pleasant folds of laudanum in order to shut out pain or doubt about Bert's faithfulness to our marriage.

One recent memory keeps surfacing even though I try to shut it out. I find it almost too painful to put into words. Last year Bert was away from home a lot and I suspected that there was another woman somewhere. Of course I never confronted him about it, but one night I heard Maidie and Bert having a heated conversation. I had gone up to bed and they obviously thought I was asleep. Their voices grew louder and louder. Eventually I got out of bed and stood at the top of the stairs in order to her what they were saying. Their conversation so devastated me that I wish I had been asleep and had not overheard it. Maidie was confronting her father: "Tell me the truth! Is what they are saying true?" She asked over and over. Bert's voice was quieter and it was much much harder for me to hear his words. Gradually I began to understand the conversation. I will write about it only briefly, because, although somehow I feel compelled to write, it is much too painful to expand on the details. Apparently, Bert has bought a house in town for a young mother with two children whose husband left her a few years ago. Bert says he did it out of kindness. Maidie says that the whole town was talking about how he is making a fool of himself. Obviously she suspects he is having an affair with this woman and I am sure that the gossip in town says the same. I am saddened by all this, but not surprised. To continue my life as it is, I have realized I cannot dwell on this.. I constantly struggle to put these events at the back of my mind. I will never tell Bert or Maidie that I overheard their conversation.

This incident makes it hard for me to concentrate on the future in any positive way. I am so tired and so afraid of illnesses yet to come. I feel as though I am recovering in my body but that my mind remains somehow trapped in the fear of pain yet to be endured. I may be a survivor but I am not strong. I try to pray for strength but my faith in God wavers. Why must I suffer constantly?

January 24, 1959

I must try to write. I know the end is near. I am very tired and in much pain, so these entries will be short and perhaps confused, although I have a few hours each day when I can think fairly clearly. I am not able to get out of bed. Bert and Lynda are so good at looking after me, so gentle and compassionate, bringing me little bits of delicious food, although I have little appetite. They sponge bathe me often, and help me out of bed to use the commode. Maidie and her girls visit almost every day, and their visits are the highlights of my days, even though I am too weak to have much conversation.

I'm upstairs in the room under the eaves which has been my private space since I decided years ago that I did not want to sleep with Bert. I know it would be so much easier for everyone if I moved down to the spare bedroom. The stairway is so narrow with that nasty turn in it, and the steps themselves are shallow to the point of being treacherous, especially if you are carrying things. But I love the privacy here and my view out over the backyard when the curtains are open, early in the morning and in the late afternoon. I can see the fields, the sunsets, the prairie grasses in the wind. I am surrounded by a few things I love, including my last my journal, with photographs and recipes tucked inside. I have often thought of burning them before I die, but now that is not possible. I cannot get downstairs on my own; in fact, even with help, I haven't been downstairs since Christmas Day. So my journals will be here after me. Why have I felt compelled to write? What is the point of it all? And yet I continue...

I feel I must try to record some of the events of what I know to be the last few months of my life or perhaps the last few weeks.

Later:

About six long weeks have passed since I last wrote. I did recover somewhat from that ruptured hernia, but I was never strong again. As I heard Bert say to several people "My darling is keeping fairly well". I think he knew that I would never return to "my old self". I have also lived these last years knowing that Bert probably has a "mistress" in town, although we never speak of it. So I will try to write of ordinary things: the farm, the family, the horses, the prairie that I love.

In 1954 and '55, the last years we had a small threshing crew, Bert took the men to the hotel for meals without even asking me about it. He and I both knew I was not well enough to cook for a crowd of hungry men who needed a lot of food quickly. Bert has now rented out most of the land, keeping only thirty acres to plant and cut himself. He has kept his vow never to have a tractor or combine on the place and still does all the work with his beloved horses.

Maidie's girls enjoy the horses; they often ride on the hay rick with Bert and sometimes, he brings Princess into the house yard for them to ride. Princess is a beautiful horse, a sorrel with a blond mane and tail. She is slightly smaller-boned than the others, which makes her a good choice for riding, although she tends to be high spirited sometimes. One summer day, I was sitting in the verandah, having tea with Maidie and watching the girls ride Princess. Bert had gone down to the barn to do some chores, as everything seemed fine. Unfortunately, the wind suddenly got gusty and as little Nora rode Princess near the swing, the wooden seat flew up and hit the horse in the rump. Princess reared and took off at a gallop. Nora fell off and lay inertly on the ground, not making a sound. Maidie rushed out and was relieved to find her conscious. Once Maidie got her standing up, she realized her left arm was broken; it was bent almost like a "V". Maidie got Nora into the car and up to the new hospital, where Dr. Kaye was able to set the arm. It healed fairly quickly, but the accident put an end to the horse back riding. Lynda-Lew is especially disappointed as she is very fond of the horses.

Maidie and the girls spent a lot of time with me, especially in the summers. Lew lost his job at Melita Lumber when Beaver Lumber took it over. They insisted it was time for him to retire although he didn't agree. At sixty seven he still wanted to work and probably was capable of doing so, but he was given no choice. He was very unhappy and Maidie worried for a while about how they would get by financially. Fortunately, she was able to get a good job in the Town Office; in fact, she is the only employee there. As Secretary-Treasurer she is responsible for keeping all the books, collecting taxes, taking minutes at Council meetings, and doing many other tasks involved in running a small town. She's good at her job, and I think that the mayor is glad to have her working there. It was fortunate that she got the job because in the fall of 1955, Lew went into Brandon Hospital for what was supposed to be a rather routine prostate operation. Apparently, the surgeon who did the operation didn't realize that Lew had diabetes. There were complications, and Lew died during the operation. A terrible shock to us all because even though Lew was 70 he was a strong and robust man who had handled his diabetes well with insulin for most of his life. Maidie was sad and wanted to shield the girls from as much grief as possible. She decided they should not go to the funeral and so they stayed with me that day. Lynda-Lew was ten; the twins were eight. I think now that Maidie's decision may have been the wrong one, although I did not tell her so at the time. I hope that when I die, Maidie will bring them to the funeral. Of course they are older now; Lynda-Lew is a teenager and the twins soon will be. We have seven grandchildren now as Kay had another boy on January 7, 1953. They were home last summer and I was well enough to really enjoy their visit. Ken at four is a sturdy happy child, a little on the roly-poly side. The girls teased him, calling him "Baby Dumpling". He really disliked that name and would come running to his mother and me for comfort. I loved cuddling with him when he climbed up on my lap!

Last fall I began to feel very weak and had to spend most days in bed. Dr. Kaye finally diagnosed my illness as shingles. This disease has been around for a long time, but Dr. Kaye explained that it is just in the last two or three years that medical research has shown the severity of the disease. I have most of the symptoms: excruciating pain, sore and itchy rashes, fever, and extreme fatigue caused by sleepless nights. I have blisters on the entire left side of my body which makes sleeping difficult. I am also light-sensitive; if the curtains in the room are open during the main part of the day, I get serious migraines. I have finally consented to move downstairs as I can not longer enjoy the view from the upstairs bedroom. I live in near darkness most of the time, although of course I have the lamp on beside my bed as I write this.

Later.... not sure of the date....

I did get out of bed for Christmas dinner when Bunny, Oscar, and Michael were home. Maidie and the girls were here as well of course and everyone tried their best to have a good time. I could tell, though, that they were all worried about me. I heard Bert whisper to Bunny: "She's bearing up, but her spirit seems broken." He was so right: my spirit is broken and it will not be repaired. Dr. Kaye gives me pain killers and sleeping pills which help my body endure but do nothing for my spirit. I am tired, tired of the pain, tired of life. No more laudanum. It's no longer used, so Dr. Kaye tells me. He also tells me I'll be better by spring but I don't believe him. I can tell by the sadness and worry in their faces that my family doesn't believe him either. I have a bad cough now and am often so racked by coughing fits that I feel my ribs are breaking. The blisters and the rashes and the sleeplessness continue. I long to rest!

I have thought seriously of saving my pills so that I could choose to end the pain permanently, but Maidie and Lynda have decided to monitor my medication and have taken the bottles away from me. Lynda came right after the new year to help look after me and she brings my pills in the correct dosage several times a day. She and Bert are so good at looking after me. Maidie and the girls come often and I try to show my appreciation and my love for them all, but I am often too tired to care if they are with me or not.

Later still...

I know that I today I have to find the courage to get out of bed and down the stairs to hide this last journal. Both Bert and Lynda have gone to town on a shopping trip, something they rarely do together. I have an hour or so by myself and I am going to get out of bed and carefully creep down to the cellar to hide this last journal with the others in the dusty, dark corner shelf in the cold room. I would prefer to burn all my journals, but of course I don't have the time or strength for that. I am too tired to write more but I am determined to use my last bit of strength in this life to hide this precious journal from prying eyes. I have already taken out the photographs and recipes and put them in a dresser drawer. I know the my daughters and their children will find them and treasure them. Who may find these books? Will they be readable? My private inner thoughts, so closely guarded all these years. Memories float by.... Bert's blue eyes, our horses, orange flashes of prairie lilies, my girls' faces as babies, as toddlers, as adults, my beloved grandchildren.

Epilogue

Nell Townsend (nee Clarke) died on February 28, 1959. She was at home on the farm, with Bert and her eldest daughter, Lynda, at her side. Bert was holding her hand as he whispered his good byes.

Bert continued to live in the house on the the farm after Nell's death. He rented the crop land to Larry Townsend, the grandson of his brother Len, who had continued to farm on the section to the north. He had his faithful border collie Spitfire for company until the end. Some of his beloved horses had died; he eventually sold the rest. He kept a couple of meat cows, did a bit of haying, had a small garden, and collected eggs from half a dozen chickens. He leased the 80 acres closest to town to the Melita Golf Club for a nine hole golf course which was built along the creek. Bert spent many hours during the last years of his life golfing for free; he walked at least some of the course every day from May to October, using only a nine iron and a putter.

Bert Townsend died on May 14, 1970. His daughter Maidie checked on him with a short visit every day. She found him lying in the cellar in the dark and phoned Dr. Kaye, who came immediately. Bert's death certificate states he died of heart failure.

The family continued to own the farm for another ten years but it was eventually sold and the proceeds divided among the seven grandchildren. Bert's dream of a son or grandson continuing the Townsend tradition on the farm was not to be.

****

Nell was my maternal grandmother. She died on the eve of my fourteenth birthday. I remember her as a frail and loving woman who kept her distance, even from her grandchildren. I did not know her as well as I would have liked. Of course, like many of us as we grow older, I have regrets about unasked questions. If only I had been more inquisitive while my mother and my aunts were alive. There is so much more I'd like to know about their childhoods on the farm.

As children, my sisters Jane and Nora and I spent a lot of time "in the valley", as we called our grandparents' farm. By that time, our grandparents were in their sixties, and we called them Nana and Dodo. We soon realized that although "Nana" was a common term, "Dodo" was not. Our friends would laugh at us when we said "Dodo". According to them "Dodo" meant "a stupid person". our grandfather was definitely not stupid. We began using the term only within the safety zone of our family and when we were speaking to Dodo directly.

Our house in town was located just a short distance from the farm in the valley. We loved the adventure of walking down the hill to see Nana and Dodo. The road descended quite steeply and in spring a small creek ran across it at the bottom. We had to cross this rushing water in our rubber boots or sometimes on a narrow, wobbly bridge made with two boards. We loved that part! In winter, Dodo often transported us in the hayrick pulled by two of our favourite horses. Those are my fondest memories, cuddled in a blanket, snuggled down in the hay, fascinated by moonlight glistening on snow, tiny bells tinkling on the horses' bridles.

When I returned to the valley as an adult, I was surprised to find that the hill was not nearly as precipitous as it had been in my childhood and the rushing water was nothing but a trickle. However, the farm has remained for me a very special place. The landscape of the prairies, the wind, the far horizons, are indelibly etched into my mind in spite of many years of living in the mountains of British Columbia.

When I began writing this book, I started it a a fictionalized version of my grandmother's life. However, as I continued to write, Nana's voice seemed to be with me. I changed to a first person point of view and began to write the book as a series of journal entries. As far as I know, Nana never kept a journal. As I wrote, I became my grandmother. I wrote down her thoughts and feelings, making up things as I went along. Nell's thoughts recorded here are mine, although one can never be sure. Perhaps some of the thoughts *are* hers, floating down through the generations, an invisible thread like a magic spider web. Or perhaps there *is* a chance that her journals were destroyed, still in their secret hiding place in the cellar when the house and barns were demolished after Bert's death. Nana was not addicted to laudanum, although she depended heavily on sleeping pills in the last two years of her life.

My own voice grew stronger as I recorded the part of Nana's life that I shared with her. Our times swimming in the creek, picking off the leeches. Sleigh rides on winter nights in 30 below weather. Did Nana participate in these activities? I think I remember her beside me. I tried not to lose her voice as I recorded those last years and the sadness she felt at the end of her life.

****

Much of the factual information in this book is taken from Bert Townsend's unpublished memoirs. In 1959, shortly after Nana's death, he spent many hours at his desk, scratching away with a pencil on long sheets of foolscap. He had kept a daily journal, recording factual information in little black notebooks, mainly about weather, crops grain prices, gardening. He was able to refer to these to pack his memoirs with interesting facts about the daily life of a farmer on the prairies during the first half of the twentieth century. However, in his memoirs, he also recorded events of a personal nature: family celebrations, humorous incidents, the birth of his four daughters, Nell's many illnesses. I have written about many of the same things here, although I have looked at them from my grandmother's perspective, or perhaps I should say, from a woman's perspective.

I typed my grandfather's memoirs for him shortly after he wrote them. I was sixteen at the time. Working on this project together made me feel very close to Dodo. Even at sixteen, I sensed that he was a complicated man and that my grandparents' marriage had been a difficult relationship. Throughout his memoirs, my grandfather always referred to Nell as "My Darling" and he constantly mentioned that they loved each other until the end.

However, there is much disagreement in our family about Bert Townsend. Some see him as a womanizer and as a man who treated Nana badly for years. Others, including my mother and I, knew him as a kind and compassionate man. The truth may lie somewhere in the middle.

"The Journals of Nell Clarke" recognizes that the margins between truth and fiction, and between reality and imagination are nebulous. It contains the imagined thoughts of my grandmother, a woman whose impulses and actions were products of a special time and place; a woman who left home and family to travel half way across the world to be with the man she loved.

Acknowledgements

"The Secret Journals of Nell Clarke" evolved over many years. Thanks to Marilyn McAllister and Carole Landry in Sorrento, BC who listened patiently and offered much encouragement in the early years of this project. My writing group in La Manzanilla, Mexico was also extremely supportive. Our regular Saturday morning meetings at Martin's restaurant inspired me to keep at this project. I am very fortunate to be part of such a talented group of writers. A special thanks to my good friend Pamala Page of Saturna Island whose thoughtful comments during our weekly Face Time editing sessions contributed so much to this book. Finally, thanks to our son Patrick Earley who has guided me in the final stages of submitting the manuscript for publication.

Journal Four: Sketch of Townsend Valley farmhouse by Nora Davidson

Journal Five: Photograph of the barn in winter by Jane Davidson

Sketch of Horses on p.151 by Lynda Earley

Cover image of Nell Clarke: Mixed media painting by Lynda Earley"

Historical reference
   Our First Century 1884 - 1984
   Melita-Arthur History Committee
   Melita, Manitoba, 1983